GATHER MY HORSES

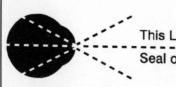

GATHER MY HORSES

JOHN D. NESBITT

THORNDIKE PRESS
A part of Gale, Cengage Learning

GALE
CENGAGE Learning·

Detroit • New York • San Francisco • New Haven, Conn • Waterville, Maine • London

GALE
CENGAGE Learning·

Thorndike Press® Large Print Western.
The text of this Large Print edition is unabridged.
Other aspects of the book may vary from the original edition.
Set in 16 pt. Plantin.

LIBRARY OF CONGRESS CATALOGING-IN-PUBLICATION DATA

Nesbitt, John D.
    Gather my horses / by John D. Nesbitt. — Large print ed.
      p. cm. — (Thorndike Press large print western)
    ISBN-13: 978-1-4104-4680-0 (hardcover)
    ISBN-10: 1-4104-4680-8 (hardcover)
    1. Western stories. gsafd I. Title.
PS3564.E76G38 2012
813'.54—dc23   2011048997

Published in 2012 by arrangement with Leisure books, a division of Dorchester Publishing Co.

For Michael Kearns, long-time friend of
the high trails.

CHAPTER ONE

As he came around a curve in the trail, swaying with the motion of his horse, Tom Fielding caught a view of the valley below the rim. Up here on top, the earth was ocher-colored, dotted with sparse vegetation and small rocks. Past the edge, the valley stretched out in dark hues of waving green. Across the sea of grass, the hills to the west rose in lighter tones, still green, while beyond them in the distance, the Laramie Mountains stood in shades of bluish gray and light purple, with patches of darkest green. Another turn in the trail closed off most of the view as the edge of the rim slanted upward. A minute later, the trail turned to the left again and began its descent, a gentle slope that led into an opening in the wall. Thirty yards ahead, the trail fell away in sharper decline, down through a gash in the bluffs. Fielding drew his horse to a stop and paused on the verge before going down.

He turned in the saddle and looked back as the first four packhorses came to a stop. The kid Mahoney had come to a halt as well, and the three pack animals he was leading bunched up behind him. Fielding motioned with his head toward the trail through the gap, and Mahoney nodded.

After a moment's breather, Fielding nudged his saddle horse and started forward. The trail itself was wide enough for wagon travel, but late spring rains had washed trenches in the road, and the horses had to pick their feet up and set them down with care as they shifted and sidestepped. By habit, Fielding held the lead rope at his hip.

Though the ruts called for careful navigation, Fielding didn't mind them. Until someone could get a team and a scraper up here, the only way to get by was on horseback, so a bit of business had come his way, packing supplies to a couple of ranches and farms up on the flats. It had been an easy trip, with not a single tree or rock for a horse to rub a pack against, and the kid Mahoney had gotten an introduction into this line of work.

Fielding glanced down at the ravine on his left, a deep cut in the yellowish earth where dark green cedars grew in the bottom and back up in a couple of clefts. Then the trail straightened out and the valley came into full view.

Straight ahead lay an expanse of grassland that sloped down toward darker grass. Beyond the meadowlike area, Chugwater Creek marked its course with a procession of trees, left to right, as the creek flowed northward to the Laramie River. Past the creek a half mile or so lay the town of Umber, which at this distance looked like three and a half rows of packing crates set along the railroad. The tracks themselves caught a shine from the afternoon sun as they ran parallel to the creek, through the center of the valley.

Fielding's gaze traveled from the middle distance out to the edge and around. Off to the south, two tree lines showed where Hunter Creek flowed into Chugwater Creek. Between those two protecting groves of cottonwoods would lie the headquarters of the Buchanan Ranch. Straight ahead across the valley, where the hills began to lift, he could pick out Bill Selby's place marked by a pale clump of trees. Farther back in the hills and up a ways, Andrew Roe's buildings squatted in a corner made by two hills. Even farther and to the left, in a place he could not see from here, would be Richard Lodge's hardscrabble claim that he called the Magpie. Then swinging his view around to the right and following the treetop course of Chugwater Creek about five miles north, Fielding picked out the site of J. P. Cronin's ranch, the Argyle.

These were his reference points as he took in the valley as a whole — the creek, the town, the railroad, and the ranches big and little in the country that spread out all around. Less distinct for him was a spot on Antelope Creek, tucked away on the other side of the far line of hills. It wasn't much as he pictured it, just a set of pole corrals, a large spreading cottonwood, a level area where he pitched his camp, and a grassy creek bottom where he turned out his horses. He couldn't rightly call it his because it was on the public domain, with no fences or boundaries to separate it from the rest of the open range; but it was his base, the place he left and returned to when he went on pack trips.

Fielding brought his attention back to the trail as his weight shifted with the horse. He had come almost to the bottom of the steep part, and the ravine on his left opened up like the mouth of a small canyon. On the far edge stood a thicket of chokecherry bushes, leafed out and grazed across the bottom like so many trees in cow country. The earth all around the thicket, except on the uphill side, was worn bare where cattle took to the shade.

Behind him he could hear the horses coming down the last part of the grade, thirty-some hooves swishing in the soft earth, nicking on stones, as the horses heaved and snorted. Fielding looked back and appreciated the procession, rocking and jostling, sometimes lurching as a hoof slipped, but orderly all the same.

The kid Mahoney rode easy, the reins in his left hand and the lead rope in his right. The young man had reddish brown hair and a light, freckled complexion, and the upturned brim of his hat did not keep the sun off his face as he turned in the saddle and gazed off to the northwest.

At the bottom where the trail leveled out, Fielding stopped the animals to let them rest for a couple of minutes. All the packs were riding even, which was to be expected, as they carried nothing but ropes, empty cloth and burlap sacks, folded canvas, and the camp items. Out of habit, Fielding counted the packhorses.

Mahoney rode up alongside and stopped. He pulled on the tag and string that hung out of the pocket of his black vest, and out came the bag of makin's. After giving the lead rope a couple of dallies around his saddle horn, he kept the reins in his left hand as he went about rolling a cigarette. He narrowed his blue-green eyes, which never seemed to be open all the way, and paid close attention to his work. He rolled a tight one, licked the free edge, and tapped the seam. Then he popped a match, held it to the end of the quirly, and drew a deep lungful of smoke. Ten seconds later he exhaled, with his head tipped again toward the northwest.

"Horses are all takin' this trip real good," he said, wrinkling his round nose and turning halfway around to look backward on his left.

"Uh-huh." Fielding thought the kid had become pretty knowledgeable in a short while. Give him a couple more days, and he'd be telling the boss how to throw his hitches and pull the slack.

Mahoney turned to his normal position without looking at Fielding. He took another drag on his cigarette and fixed a hard glance at the valley, as if it were going to yield to his scrutiny.

Fielding took a deep breath to keep himself from getting impatient. He told himself

Mahoney was just a green kid trying to prove himself. From the looks of him, he had just gotten his new outfit a short while back in Cheyenne. His round-crowned hat, striped shirt, denim trousers, and brown boots were all close to brand-new. So were his nickel-plated spurs with one-inch rowels, and so was his .44 with the clean wooden grips and the new bluing. Just a kid with a fuzzy mustache.

Fielding waited until Mahoney finished his cigarette. Then he put his horse into motion and looked back. The other horses no doubt knew they were on the way home, as they picked up their feet and jogged along. Mahoney fell in behind with his three horses, and the little pack train moved in order as before.

The group stopped in town long enough for Fielding to leave off the mail he had brought down from the flats and for Mahoney to water the horses. When Fielding came out of the little wooden building that housed the post office, he saw the kid slouched by the water trough, a cigarette drooping from his lips and his right thumb on his gun belt. His left hand held the ropes for the two strings of pack animals, and the saddle horses were hitched to the rack. Fielding gave an upward toss of the head as

13

he moved to untie his horse, and when he had the reins, the kid handed him a lead rope. Fielding led his horse out, checked the cinch, and swung aboard. The afternoon sun had still not dipped below the tip of his hat brim when he crossed the tracks and headed westward.

Traveling light as he was, he figured he could cover the four miles to his campsite in less than an hour. If he were pressed for time and riding alone, he might save from a quarter to a half hour by straightening out the route rather than follow the trail as it wound through the low hills. But he had no reason to hurry today. He was on the tail end of an easy trip, with plenty of daylight left.

After the first curve in the trail and going into the second, which set the course westward again, Fielding saw the light green shades of box elder and young cottonwoods that marked Bill Selby's place. Fielding had seen it from across the valley and up a ways, but from the valley floor to here, swells in the rising land closed off all but the fringe of the treetops. Now the ranch site came into view, a quarter of a mile to the left.

It looked as if Selby had company. He was facing three men who stood by their horses. The men had their backs to the lane that came in from the main trail.

Fielding gave the scene a close study as his horse clip-clopped along. A feeling of displeasure rose within him as he noted the layout. Selby stood hatless in the middle of his ranch yard, face-to-face with a larger man in a dark shirt. From this distance, the man looked like George Pence, one of J. P. Cronin's riders and not the most likeable. The other two men were standing back holding the horses, with not much more than their hats visible.

A voice rose on the air as the man in the dark shirt made a flicker of movement. Fielding tensed, then reined his horse to the left and nudged him to follow the lane into the yard. Fielding glanced back to see that Mahoney was following, caught a curious look from the kid, and turned forward to keep things on course. As he approached the ranch yard, the men and horses stood ahead on his right.

Another voice came up, followed by the loud one. Fielding rode closer, wondering when the men in the yard would hear the footfalls of the nine horses.

As the voices died away, one of the two men holding the visitors' horses came around the front of the nearest one and stared at the oncoming party. He was a

15

clean-shaven man, a little taller than average. He wore a brown hat, brown vest, and white shirt. Fielding strained to try to recognize the man, but he saw nothing familiar about him.

The horses moved on, thirty-six hooves clopping and scuffing. The man in the brown vest raised his head in an expression of authority, then spoke over his shoulder to the large man facing Selby.

The scene ahead shifted, and the large man came to stand next to his associate. Fielding recognized the tall-crowned hat, dark blue wool shirt, beefy face, and brown side whiskers. It was George Pence, just as he had thought at first glance.

As Fielding brought his horse to a stop, the man in the brown vest spoke. His words had an even tone, neither friendly nor menacing.

"Afternoon, stranger. What's your business?"

Fielding dismounted. He didn't like to ride into someone's camp or ranch and look down on him, just as he didn't like another man to act that way toward him. "Not a stranger," he said, passing the reins to his right hand. "Don't need to be on business to drop in and see a friend." He motioned with his head in the direction of Selby, who had come forward but stood a few paces away from the other two.

The brown hat nodded. "We're all friends," said the man. "That's what we stopped in for. A friendly visit."

Fielding noted the smooth voice, the polite accent he had heard in others who affected a gentleman's image. "That's good," he said, "for everyone to be friends." He flicked a glance at the blocky form of George Pence, met his dull brown eyes, and came back to the clean-shaven man with the clean vest and white shirtsleeves. "My name's Tom Fielding, and I'm a packer."

The other man smiled without showing his teeth. "I like a man who says what he is." The dark eyes traveled down the file of horses and came back. "And I like a man who is what he says." Another smile. "My name's Al Adler. I'm the foreman at J. P. Cronin's Argyle Ranch." The man pulled a brown leather glove off his right hand and offered to shake.

Fielding obliged, noticing that the firm hand was pale and the fingernails were clean. "Pleasure to meet you."

"All mine." Adler tossed his head sideways and said, "I would guess you already know George Pence."

Fielding nodded in the direction of the

big man, whose eyelids halfway closed as he nodded back.

"And here's Henry in back. Do you know him, too?"

Fielding looked across the saddles of the first two horses and caught a smile and a wave from Henry Steelyard. "How do, Henry?"

"Howdy, Tom."

Adler's smooth voice came out again. "So, as I was saying, we were all just having a friendly visit."

"Sure." Fielding turned toward Selby. "And how are you today, Bill?"

Selby's ruddy face was redder than usual, but he said, "Good enough, I suppose."

Adler's voice cut in. "Did you have any business with Mr. Selby? Any goods to deliver?"

"No more business than I already stated." Fielding tipped his head toward his packhorses. "I'm travelin' empty, back to my camp."

"Well, don't let us keep you, then" said Adler. After half a pause he added, "Who's your man?"

Fielding followed the glance of the dark eyes. "That's Fred Mahoney. This is his first job with me."

Mahoney, who had not gotten down from

his horse, raised his hand from the saddle horn in a small wave.

Adler's eyes rested on Fielding again. "Like I said, don't let us keep you."

"Oh, we're not in a hurry."

"Maybe you ought to be," said Pence.

The surly tone was nothing new to Fielding, who felt a spark of resentment. "I said I wasn't."

Pence stepped forward and squared his shoulders. His right hand hung over his smooth-worn gun belt. "Maybe we think you should. You interrupted a conversation, you know."

Fielding cast a glance at Selby. "Is that right, Bill?"

Selby's voice seemed to have a quaver in it as he answered. "I suppose so, in a way. Pence here was trying to tell me where to run my cattle, or where not to. I said it was open range, and his boss didn't have any more right to it than I do."

Pence cut in. "That's a mealymouthed way of puttin' it. What I said was, he'd better keep his rib-racked cattle off the Argyle meadows."

Selby came right back, his voice steadier now. "And I told him that if any of that land was private, it was up to the owner to fence it off. That's Wyoming law, and everyone

19

knows it."

The big man made a sound like "Pah."

Selby's jaw muscles tightened, and his eyes blazed. "They just came here to bully me. They ride in here, the three of them, and they put this one on me like a bulldog."

Pence made a quick turn and, with spurs jingling, moved toward Selby, who backed up. "Stand still," barked Pence, "and take what you've got comin'."

Selby's blue eyes flickered from one side to the other as he took another step backward. He was short and sturdy, but no match for the larger man. "Just a bully," he said. "All the courage in the world when you've got someone three to one."

Pence doubled his fists, and his voice came out gravelly as he said, "I'll take you one on one." He moved forward.

Fielding dropped his reins, took about five quick steps, and came between the two men with his shoulder almost touching Pence's chest. "I think that's enough," he said. "There's no need for any more."

Pence laid his left hand on Fielding's shoulder and gave him a shove. "This pissy little nester called me a bully."

Fielding squared around. "Maybe you are. Look at you. And you're callin' names just as much as he is."

20

The big man surged forward and shoved Fielding with both hands, throwing him off balance but not knocking him down. Fielding went back a couple of steps, regained his footing, and got ready for the other man as he came hulking toward him. As long as it was just a shoving match, Fielding did not want to throw a punch. He hovered with his weight forward, and then he pushed off.

He went between Pence's two hands, which were poised above waist level and were not yet tensed for another shove. The thumbs gave way. Grabbing the big man by the shirt and putting the toe of his boot on Pence's right spur, Fielding pushed hard and sent the man backward, arms flailing for balance. Pence landed with his butt on the ground, and his high-crowned hat went rolling away. His pale forehead showed where his dark brown curly hair was receding. As he turned in a smooth motion and came up with his .45 Colt, the beginning of a bald spot showed in back.

Adler stepped in to block Pence's view, though the barrel of the six-gun was still raised in Fielding's direction.

"This has gone far enough," said the foreman. "Put it away, George."

Fielding, having stepped out of the line of fire, saw the gun barrel lower and withdraw.

Adler turned to Fielding. "Maybe I'll say it a third time, my friend. Don't let us keep you from going on your way."

Fielding gave him a cross look. "So you can pick on Bill some more?"

Adler jutted his chin and shook his head. "No one's pickin' on anybody. We're about to leave, too. That's the secret of a friendly visit, know when to leave so you don't stay too long."

Fielding turned to Selby, who was standing off by himself with his hands at his sides. "Are you all right, Bill?"

"Oh, I'll be fine." Selby had a subdued tone, but he did not seem afraid. His eyes followed Pence, who had gotten up and found his hat and was now walking back to the horses.

Fielding shrugged. "I guess we'll go, then."

Adler raised his eyebrows. "All the best." Then after giving a closemouthed smile, he added, "Good to meet you, Fielding."

"The same here." Fielding returned to his horse, a calm sorrel that stood hipshot with its head forward. Fielding gathered the reins, turned the sorrel, and found the lead rope for the first packhorse where it lay in the dirt. Positioning the sorrel to avoid throwing his leg over the lead rope when he swung aboard, Fielding held the reins and

22

the rope at the saddle horn as he mounted up. He transferred the reins to his right hand, and with his left he waved to Bill Selby and Henry Steelyard.

Adler was turning out his stirrup and had his back to Fielding, as did Pence in his dark hat. That was just as well, thought Fielding. As he turned the packhorses and led the way out of the yard, he looked across at Mahoney, who had not gotten down from his horse the whole time and who gave no expression in response. That was just as well, too.

The campsite on the west side of Antelope Creek was a welcome sight as Fielding brought the pack train in off the trail. He and Mahoney worked together to untie the packs, lift the panniers off the sawbucks, strip the gear, and water the horses. They picketed two, a dun and a gray, then belled the rest of the packhorses and turned them loose. They tied the two saddle horses to the corral for the time being.

Next they set up two tents, using the poles that Fielding had left stacked. They set up one tent for living quarters and one to stow the gear, including the tepee tent they had used on their recent trip. When they had the gear put away, Fielding stood back and looked over the whole layout.

"I think that's pretty good," he said, turning to Mahoney. "If you want, we can call it a day." He brought out a ten-dollar gold piece and handed it to the young man. "Here's this. We can call it square for the six days."

Mahoney's eyebrows went up. "Thanks," he said.

Fielding waved toward the corral. "Go ahead and take the horse you've been riding. You can leave him at the livery stable in town, and I'll pick him up when I go in. Probably tomorrow."

Mahoney nodded, turned to walk toward the brown horse, and stopped. Someone was riding into the camp from the main trail.

As the horse came to a stop about twenty-five yards out, Fielding recognized the features of the young range rider. "Come on in, Henry," he called.

Steelyard rode his horse another fifteen yards and then dismounted. Leading the animal by the reins, he walked forward with his usual easy air about him. His round hat with the ranger's peak was set back on his head, and his trimmed, wavy brown hair combined with his clean-shaven face to give him a look of innocence.

"Evenin', Henry. What brings you to this side of the valley?"

"Oh, I just thought I'd drop by to see if everything was all right."

"I hope so."

"That's good. You know, I felt kinda awkward, bein' in the middle of that scrape earlier in the afternoon."

Fielding waved his hand. "Ah, don't worry about it. I didn't think you had anything to do with it."

Steelyard shrugged. "Well, I was there, and I wouldn't want to have any hard feelin's."

"None on this side, not towards you. As for Pence — well, I'll just have to wait and see if he wants to start somethin' again. You know as well as I do that some of these things go away on their own, and some don't."

Steelyard pushed out his lower lip. "I don't blame you for steppin' in," he said. His words hung on the air until he added, "But I don't know how good an idea it would be to take sides."

Fielding's eyebrows pulled together. "What do you mean, take sides?"

"I didn't say you did." Steelyard laid his hand out, palm up. "I meant something you might or might not do later on."

"Such as . . ."

"Better not to burn bridges." Steelyard gave a tip of the head.

"Ah, as far as that goes, I figure I already lost any work I thought I might have with Cronin."

"Well, that, or anything else. Just thought I'd mention it." The young man's brown eyes were steady.

"I'm glad you did. Good of you to drop by."

Steelyard gave a backward wave. "Think nothin' of it." He glanced at the sun, which was about to set. "Huh," he said, "looks like I'd better be headin' back."

"Are you goin' by way of town?"

"I could. Do you need somethin' done?"

Fielding motioned toward Mahoney, who had been standing by and taking things in. "I don't, but Mahoney here was about to leave. He could ride along if it was no bother to you."

Steelyard looked at Mahoney and smiled. "Not at all. Glad for the company. Was your name Pat?"

"Fred."

"Good enough. Well, I'm ready to go when you are."

Mahoney untied the brown horse, led it out a few yards, tightened the cinch, and mounted up. Steelyard swung aboard also, and the two young men waved good-bye and rode away.

As the hoofbeats faded on the trail, Fielding unsaddled the sorrel and put him in the corral. He gave the animal a bait of grain and went to look for a canvas bucket. When he came out of the gear tent holding the bucket by its rope handle, he paused to appreciate the sunset over the skyline. Shades of orange and scarlet shot through a layer of low-lying clouds, and the rangeland was falling into shadow.

The bells of the grazing horses tinkled in the still air, and the creek made a light, rippling sound as Fielding walked toward it. He washed his hands and face in the stream, then dipped the bucket and brought it up swelled and dripping.

Night was falling as he walked to his camp. It was a good feeling to have the day's work done, a night horse close at hand, a bucket of water to hang in camp, and no one to mar the pleasure of being alone on the plain.

CHAPTER TWO

The buzzing of a fly woke him. As he opened his eyes, he realized the sun was up and warming the tent. The light music of the horse bells floated on the air, and he thought of the old saying. Bell your horses and sleep good.

He rolled out of bed, got dressed, and went out in the morning. The sorrel snuffled in the corral. Fielding put a lead rope on him, led him out, and went to untie the two picket horses. The sun was warm on his face as he led the three horses to water. The young cottonwoods on the opposite bank cast the stream in shadow, and the cool smell of morning lingered. The horses touched their muzzles to the surface and made their small sucking sounds as they drank their water upward. A magpie chattered from the big cottonwood near camp.

Fielding turned the sorrel loose and moved the pickets for the dun and the gray.

By habit he counted the loose horses, as he had done earlier, and went back to camp.

He had dipped fresh water for coffee and had the fire going when he heard the footfalls of a horse on dry ground. Looking north toward the trail, he saw Richard Lodge riding in on one of the two matched sorrels that the man kept. Fielding waved him in. Lodge came closer, then swung down and walked the last few yards.

"You can tie him to the corral or turn him in. Coffee should be ready in a few minutes."

"You're a good boy." Lodge tipped back his hat and smiled. The sunlight fell on his dark hair and graying beard. He wore a clean work shirt, drab but not wrinkled or sweat-stained, and his charcoal-colored vest was closed by one button. After a pause in his step, he walked on to the corral.

A minute later, he took a seat on one of the two lengths of old tree trunk that did for camp furniture. Fielding sat on the other, holding the rod of green willow that he used for a poker.

After a few seconds, Lodge raised his eyes from gazing at the campfire. "How's business?" he asked.

"Oh, all right. I packed some grub and a few other things up to the flats. Got back yesterday."

"That's what I heard."

"Things don't really pick up until later on, you know. Then I'll have more work than I can handle, packin' supplies to cow and sheep camps."

"Who's your helper?"

"Kid named Mahoney. Says he's from Cheyenne. I'm just tryin' him out. Maybe he's doin' the same." Fielding thought for a second. "Have you talked to Selby?"

In the shade of the camp, Lodge's deep brown eyes were darker than usual. "He said you dropped by. Raised a little dust."

"Not much."

Lodge sniffed. "Don't know if they'd've done much, but it was just as well that you showed up. Maybe saved some trouble." He tipped his head back and forth. "Then again, maybe it caused some."

"Either way, I didn't like it. Someone's better off than the rest, and he thinks he can ride roughshod over the ones that don't have much. I just don't like it."

"I don't, either, of course, bein' one of those that has less."

Fielding gave a light shake of the head. "Then their young puncher named Steelyard, nice enough fellow, comes by and tells me I ought not to take sides."

30

"He told you that?"

"I think he meant it well. He's the type that just by nature stays out of trouble. But if I did what he said, looked the other way, I'd be doing what he is, which is more or less goin' along with what Cronin does."

"I'm surprised he took the trouble to tell you."

"I am, too. He had to go out of his way to do it. I'd guess he heard something from Pence or Adler after I left, and it didn't sound good."

Lodge frowned. "That Cronin's a high-handed son of a bitch, and he hires men to do things his way."

"This is the first time I'd seen Adler. I'd heard there was a new foreman, but I didn't know what he looked like."

Lodge held his eyes on Fielding. "And what does he look like to you?"

"Oh, I don't know. He doesn't seem to be from around here."

"I think you've got that right."

"After a man's been here awhile, he takes on the look of the country," said Fielding. "His clothes weather to this climate, and he does, too."

"That's right," said Lodge. "And I don't think Cronin brought this fellow in because of his knowledge about runnin' cattle on

31

the northern range."

Fielding smiled. "You mean he doesn't look like a foreman to you."

"Not as much as some."

Fielding reflected. "You know, I didn't even notice if he was wearing a gun."

"If you see much of him, you will. And he carries a saddle gun, too. I've seen that."

"Then you think he's some kind of a —"

"The nice term is stock detective. If he hadn't hired on as foreman, he might go by that." Lodge raised his chin. "Can you get that coffeepot any closer to the coals? It's takin' a while to boil."

"I can try." Fielding took a stick of firewood, moved two rocks closer to the center of the fire, and set the coffeepot in place.

"I can tell you're not in any hurry today. You're not like these others that live on the trail — boil their coffee in a little can, and kick dirt on the ashes before the sun comes up."

Fielding smiled. "I don't have someone trailin' after me."

"That's good."

"I do need to go into town a little later on."

Lodge gazed at the fire. "Yeah, I need to go in there one of these days, too. Boy, those bells have a pretty sound, don't they?

Meadowlarks sing right along with 'em."

The talk ran on, touching on light topics. Lodge asked about the places where Fielding had been — what the grass was like, how the wheat farmers seemed to be doing, whether the snakes were out yet. When the visitor finished his cup of coffee, he stood up.

"Well, I think I'd better move on," he said. "Thanks for the coffee."

"Glad you got some. I usually boil it in a little can."

"I know." Lodge untied his horse and turned toward Fielding before mounting up. "Thanks for the help you gave Bill," he said.

"It wasn't much."

"Maybe not, but he appreciates it. Others of us do, too."

"Thanks. That's good to know."

Lodge's deep brown eyes looked away and came back. "Selby and Roe are plannin' their own roundup. I'll throw in what little I have. They could use another hand or two, if you're still in the country."

"I might be."

Lodge took the sorrel out into the sunlight, where he checked the cinch and climbed on. "Come and see me in your life of leisure," he said.

"I'll do that." Fielding watched as the

horse and rider trotted off to the south, through the grassy valley where the belled horses were grazing.

On his way to town, Fielding took a detour to the southeast. He rode a buckskin that covered the ground at a fast walk and a smooth lope, so he crossed Hunter Creek before the sun was straight up overhead. He followed a cow trail for a ways and then cut across a meadow to a grove of cottonwoods. Coming out on the other side, he picked up the lane that led into the headquarters of the Buchanan Ranch.

A short-haired terrier came off the front porch of the ranch house, barking, and did not let up until the front door opened and a young blonde woman stepped out.

Fielding's pulse quickened for a second. As the young woman called the dog to her, Fielding dismounted and led his horse forward.

Her voice had a pleasant tone to it as she said, "Good morning, Tom. I believe it's still morning, isn't it?"

"I think so. How are you, Susan?"

"Very well, thanks." As she stood in the open yard, the sunlight shone on her straw-colored hair, which was tied up in a neat coil. Her high-necked white blouse and long, sky blue skirt also caught the light and added to her radiance.

"I hope I didn't come at a bad moment."

She frowned. "Oh, no. Why?"

"I wouldn't want to interrupt your dinner hour."

She smiled, and her blue eyes sparkled. "Not at all. We won't even start until Father gets back."

"Oh, I see. Then he's not around?"

"No, he's in town. Or that's where he went. Did you wish to see him?"

Fielding gave a jaunty toss of the head. "Well, that was my main reason for stopping by. But I wouldn't want to be so blunt as to not give my best to you."

She smiled again, this time showing her pretty teeth. "It's nice of you to be so gallant, Tom."

"Thank you. I couldn't do it without inspiration." He felt himself blush and he thought she colored as well, but he couldn't be sure in the warm sunlight.

She gave a light laugh, then in her easy way moved to another topic. "I heard you went off on a delivery trip. I'm glad to see you made it back without any trouble."

"It was all pretty easy, there and back."

Silence hung between them for a few seconds. He let his eyes rove over her facial features, which were friendly but not revealing. It occurred to him that if she had heard one thing, she might have heard another.

They both went to speak at the same time, and then she laughed and said, "Go ahead."

"You first."

"No, you. I insist." She gave him a mock-severe look.

"Well," he began, "there was another little thing. You may have heard of it, and I wouldn't want you to think that I didn't want — or was trying to —"

"I think I know what you're referring to. An incident with the men from the Argyle."

"That's it. I was hoping you wouldn't —"

"Oh, don't worry for my sake, Tom. I know you wouldn't start something like that." Her words lifted and hung.

"But —" he said.

"But it's a dreadful thing to be drawn into, don't you think?"

"I suppose so," he answered, with some sense of how she might see it. "I'm just hoping I haven't put some uncomfortable distance between me and your father."

She tipped her head ever so slightly to one side. "Do you mean, for business interests?"

"For any reason. I don't want to be on bad terms with someone because of other people's squabbles."

The tension seemed to relax as she gave an assuring smile. "Tom, you know my father is a fair man."

"I know. That's why I dropped in. I felt I could."

"Of course." Now her blue eyes were both soft and direct. "But I'm sorry you got drawn into that incident."

"I just didn't like to see the bullying."

She looked down and then up at him again. "I don't blame you. I felt bad for you, and I don't want to presume to be telling you anything about it."

"Please do."

"You mean, what I think?"

"Exactly. Yes."

She hesitated, and her mouth was small and pretty. Then she said, "I do not mean for this to reflect on you at all, but it just seems to me that it's not worth it to stick up for people who probably wouldn't do the same for you."

Fielding opened his eyes wide. "Do you think your father sees it that way?"

Her face looked innocent now. "I don't know how he has considered it, but I do know that he tries to avoid entanglements."

"That's good," said Fielding, even as he wondered whether Joseph Buchanan would side with his own kind or stay aloof if things came to the point of trouble. Fielding was trying to think of the next thing to say when he heard a horse trotting into the yard behind him. Thinking it might be Mr. Buchanan himself, Fielding turned halfway and looked over his shoulder.

What he saw surprised him. A man in a light tan suit was jolting along on a cream-colored horse. He wore no hat, and his full head of hair, yellowish white like corn silk, blazed in the noonday sun. He had the reins crossed in front and held apart with both hands. As he came closer he stood in the stirrups, then sat again, still bouncing. He did not slow the horse but rode right on by, turning his flushed, perspiring face toward Susan and then glaring with pale green eyes at Fielding. Thirty yards off, he stopped the horse and dismounted in the shade of a cottonwood tree.

"Looks as if you have company," said Fielding.

Susan gave a half shrug and a nod.

"Well," he went on, pulling the reins through his right hand, "give my best to your father, if I don't see him before you do."

She smiled. "Even if you do, I'll be sure to tell him how courteous you've been."

Fielding returned the smile. "Much

obliged." Nodding toward the cottonwood, he said, "That fellow looks as if he needs a drink of water."

"I'll see to it." After a second's pause she added, "Thanks for stopping in."

"My pleasure. Hope to see you again before long." He turned the buckskin around, swung aboard, and set off. After a few paces he touched his spur to the horse, and they left the Buchanan place on a lope.

In town, Fielding went to the livery stable, paid for the day's keep, and saddled the brown horse. He put the bridle and reins in his saddlebag and led the horse by a neck rope. He had not ridden two blocks when he met Joseph Buchanan, who had just walked out of the grain dealer's office. He was putting on his tall dark brown hat with four dents in the peak, and he had his leather gloves in his left hand. Fielding reined his horse over and swung down.

"Good afternoon, Mr. Buchanan. How do you do?"

"Oh, I'm fine. And yourself?" Buchanan's dark blue eyes went from Fielding to the two horses and back.

"Fine as well." After a second's pause, he added, "I just came by your place, but I missed you."

Buchanan's eyebrows went up and down. "I was on my way home now. Anything urgent?"

"Oh, no. I was just passing by, so I stopped there. I know it might be early in the season for you, but I've already started packing, so I thought I'd let you know I'm ready whenever you might need me."

Buchanan looked at the brown horse again, stroked the underside of his jaw with his thumb and first two fingers, and cleared his throat. He was clean-shaven and had a trim mustache, but his weather-tanned face was starting to go heavy and the lines were setting in. He looked tired, as if he had to work himself up to what he had to say. He took a breath and said, "I'll tell you, Fielding, I need to take things into consideration."

"Of course."

Buchanan seemed to hesitate and then said, "I heard you had a little trouble with the Argyle men."

"Not much, but there was a small incident."

"Sure. And we don't need to go through it. You're your own man."

"Thank you, sir."

The blue eyes wandered and then came back to Fielding. "But after considering it,

40

I've had to decide that it would be better if I didn't have you transport goods for me if there was any possibility of mishaps."

"Oh, I don't think there would be, sir."

"You can't tell, but at any rate, that's what I've decided."

"I see." Fielding felt a sinking of the spirits.

Buchanan's voice, in contrast, picked up. "That doesn't mean I don't value your work. I'd be happy to put in a good word for you, any time."

"Why, thank you, sir. I appreciate that."

"Just fine, and good luck to you, boy."

"All the same to you, sir."

Buchanan turned and walked away, his heavy brown boots thumping on the board sidewalk.

Fielding led the buckskin out into the street and swung aboard again. The conversation with Buchanan had left him almost in a daze, as he had been hit by the main point when he thought he was still working up to it. Fielding thought it was polite of Buchanan to make it seem as if Cronin's men were the problem, but he could see that it was a nice piece of condescension as Buchanan cut off business with him.

Then came the second part. Fielding was left to interpret that he probably didn't have

41

much welcome at the Buchanan ranch house anymore. Now that he thought of it, Susan had not said to come back again. Fielding frowned and then shrugged. So much the better for the hatless, red-faced young gentleman.

Out on the trail, the brown horse stepped right along as the buckskin kept up a fast walk. Fielding rode past Selby's, where no activity stirred in the ranch yard. He thought that was just as well, as he didn't care to see Selby again quite so soon. A couple of miles farther, as the road curved through the rolling country, he came to Andrew Roe's place, also on his left. Thinking that it wouldn't hurt to have a word with Roe, Fielding turned in.

As he rode along the lane, he realized it was the first time he had come in from the road and had seen the layout up close. Roe had a good location for his homestead. The house and other buildings lay in a corner formed by two hills, which gave protection from the strong winds that came from the southwest, west, and northwest from November to May.

Although the place was well situated, Fielding thought a man could make better use of it. At some point, Roe had planted a windbreak of trees on the north side, but now it consisted of three rows of dead stumps. At the far end of the windbreak and a little to the left, a roofed shelter on poles had fallen in on one end and was leaning on the other. Farther to the left, the stable and then the house looked east, which made for good sunshine on winter mornings and shade on summer afternoons, but the whole front yard was littered with heaps of salvage.

Roe's accumulations had some order, as the fence posts lay in a pile next to the warped planks, the rusty barbed wire had its own mound with weeds growing up through it, the wagon parts leaned against or lay on top of a couple of crippled old spring wagons, and the scraps of curled and perforated tin roofing were held down by a rusted iron bedstead tipped on its side.

To give the man his due, Fielding reflected that Roe had not had it easy. His wife had died a few years back, and he had finished raising his daughter by himself. If the wife had been healthier or the girl had been big enough, someone might have watered the trees. The last time Fielding had seen her, a year or so back, the girl was big enough to do the cooking and cleaning. She probably did the chores as well, as Roe had a reputation for dropping in on other homesteaders or idling about town, picking up scraps of gossip along with items of perceived value. He was not very open about having people come to his place, perhaps because of the girl, but perhaps because he would rather have a bite to eat or take a nip at someone else's place and not have to return the favor. So the talk ran, at least.

Two large gray geese came around the side of the house, lifting their wings and honking. From somewhere in back a calf bawled, and the cackle of chickens rose and fell.

As Fielding stopped his horse, the front door opened. He expected to see Andrew Roe appear, rubbing his face or running his fingers through his hair, but the person who stepped outside was the girl.

Her name came to him. Isabel.

The house had no porch, but the front step lay in the first of the afternoon shadow. The girl's dark, shoulder-length hair and her dusky complexion reminded him of the little he had heard about her mother — that she had come from New Mexico and had Spanish in her background. He had not connected that information with the name Isabel until now.

"Good afternoon," he said. "I stopped in to see if your father was at home. My name's Tom Fielding, and I've got a camp a couple of miles farther out. He knows me."

The girl's dark eyes took in the rider and the two horses. Then her voice came floating from the shadow, musical as the lark's song. "He's not at home right now. You're welcome to wait for him if you'd like."

"Well, I wouldn't want to —"

"There's a trough over there, if you'd like to water your horses. It shouldn't be long."

He turned to where she pointed. A wooden trough with a hand pump stood in front of the stable. "I suppose so," he said. Holding the lead rope out of the way, he drew back his right leg and dismounted. When he came around in front of the buckskin, the girl was gone.

He led the two horses to drink, then took them back to loiter in front of the house.

The door opened again, and the girl Isabel came out carrying a three-legged stool. "Here," she said. "You can sit in the shade if you'd like."

The paint was yellowed and chipped, but the stool looked sturdy enough. "I guess I could," he said.

She took a short step down and set the stool next to the house. "I'll be back," she said.

As she stood up, Fielding appreciated her figure in the dark gray dress. Then she was gone again, and he took his seat on the stool, resting his back against the house as he held the lead rope in his left hand and the reins in his right. Both horses were relaxed, and the barnyard animals had quieted down. Though the immediate surroundings were homely, the spot had a peaceful quality to it.

The door opened, and the girl set a chair on the step. A few seconds later she returned with a cutting board, a knife, and a chunk of meat that looked like a venison haunch.

"There's not many flies yet," she said. "I thought I could work outside here."

"That's good. You can keep those geese from doin' me any harm."

She smiled and showed her clean, even teeth. "Oh, they're something, aren't they? But that's geese." With the board in her lap, she positioned the chunk of meat and sliced off a thin strip lengthwise.

"Makin' jerky?"

"That's right. It's antelope meat. Papa says they're good this time of the year, when the grass comes green." She glanced up from her work. "So, you live over this way, do you?"

"I have a camp is all. I'm a packer, so I'm on the trail a good part of the time, when the weather allows."

Her dark eyes looked at him again. "I think we've met. Or seen each other. I'm Isabel, you know."

He took off his hat, but she didn't seem to notice the courtesy, so he dragged his cuff across his forehead. "And I'm Tom, as I already mentioned."

"Sure." She pulled the knife through the haunch and cut off a long, thin piece. "I think Bill Selby mentioned you just yesterday when he came by."

Fielding shifted on his stool. "It was a little thing that happened, but everyone seems to have heard of it."

"I think Bill came over here to tell Papa just as soon as he could. He made you out to seem like the rescuer."

"Like I say, it wasn't much."

She paused in her work and let her eyes meet his. "Do you think those other men mean trouble? Bill seemed shaken by it."

Fielding rotated his hat in his hands. "I don't know what all they said before or after I was there. I just saw them pushin' him around, and I didn't think it was fair. If there's something bigger behind it, I'm yet to know."

"But you stuck your neck out. That's what Bill said. I know he appreciated it."

"I'm glad he did. I don't think the other

47

side did, though."

"But you stood up for him, see? That's good."

He felt relaxed with her, and his words came easy. "Oh, I don't know. I think I'm just innocent enough to believe that there are still things like right and wrong and that decency can come out on top. It's just that it's hard to do without causing some kind of friction."

She cut another long slice, then flipped it to the side with her knife. "You've got to do what you think is right. You've got to be your own man." She looked across at him and smiled.

"Well, you're right, of course. What I want is to be left alone, free to live the way I want, but like I say, I tend to make it rough on myself."

"Maybe you do, a little bit. But I'd rather do that and be able to be myself, not have a lot of people hanging all over me." Her voice changed tone as she said, "Don't worry about her."

"Huh?"

Isabel pointed with her knife, and Fielding turned to see a young brown goat, about a yearling, with bulging yellow eyes.

"She likes tobacco."

"Well, I don't have any."

The young nanny looked at Fielding's shirt, then at the two horses.

"Go away, Missy," said Isabel. "No treats today."

The goat stood still.

Isabel spoke again as she returned to her work. "So, do you always travel with two horses?"

"Um, no."

"I don't mean to be inquisitive. Just something to talk about." She looked up, and her dun complexion had a blush. "Really, I talk too much. But just at first. Hardly anyone ever comes here, and if they do, it's like Bill Selby. They come to talk to Papa."

"And give tobacco to the goat?"

Isabel laughed.

Fielding realized the girl might be a little nervous or giddy about having a visitor like him, but he felt an easy familiarity with her. He said, "Anyway, to answer your question, the reason I look like Ranger Two Ponies is that I picked up this one horse where my helper left it in town."

"Oh, I see. And you're taking it back to your place." Her voice was calmer now.

"Unless something comes up."

She looked at him without raising her head all the way. "Oh, are you a horse

49

trader, too?"

"No, but the world is full of genies and spirits, and one of them might bewitch me."

Her eyes sparkled as she smiled at him. "Like sailors and mermaids."

He smiled back. "Maybe so. I've heard it said that a cowpuncher is a sailor on horseback."

"So, you're a cowpuncher?"

"I've done that kind of work."

She tipped her head in a matter-of-fact way. "I like to ride," she said. Then, as if emending, she added, "But that's nothing like cow-punching, I know that. You have to ride long and hard, know how to rope and trip steers, keep from breaking your neck."

"That, and live on cold biscuits. Boil your coffee in a little can."

She pursed her lips. "And jerky."

"Oh, I know," he conceded. "A fella carries raisins, dried apples, canned tomatoes. I was just makin' myself to be a lone sufferer for the moment."

"I'm sure it's not easy." Her voice changed again. "Well, what did I tell you? Here's Papa now."

Fielding followed the motion of her head toward the east, where Andrew Roe on horseback came down a grassy hill. Fielding recognized the horse, an older chestnut that did not move very fast. Fielding stood up and put on his hat.

Isabel resumed her work, and neither she nor Fielding spoke as her father made his way to the ranch yard.

Andrew Roe stopped his horse. "Been here long?" he asked as he eased down from the saddle.

"Not long," said Fielding. "Ten, fifteen minutes."

Isabel rose from her chair and carried the cutting board with the knife and meat into the house.

"What news?" asked Roe. He stood by the horse as it drooped its head. The man was of medium height and slender build, and he wore loose clothes. His hat had nicks in the brim and a hole worn in the ridge of the crown, and it cast a shadow on his eyes, which in turn had permanent shadows below them. As usual, the man had a couple of days' stubble on his face, set off by a knotted kerchief that could use a wash.

"Not much news from me," said Fielding. "Least, nothin' you haven't heard."

Roe said something like "Yuh" and moistened his lips. His pale brown eyes, which had a tendency to drift, came back to Fielding. "I was just over to Selby's now," he went on. "Talkin' about work."

" 'Bout that time."

Roe moved his mouth and then spoke. "Him and me, we're thinkin' of havin' our own roundup."

"I believe Lodge mentioned something like that when I saw him."

Isabel came out the front door. She walked forward, took the reins from her father, and led the horse away.

Roe dug into the pocket of his cloth vest and brought out a sack of tobacco. He looked down at his work as he spoke. "The Association doesn't control that anymore, so no one can tell us otherwise. A couple of others might throw in with us — you mentioned Lodge — and we'd like to have another hand or two." Roe twisted his mouth as he rolled the cigarette tight with his fingers. Then he licked the edge and folded it down.

When the man seemed to have his attention free, Fielding answered, "Lodge mentioned that, too. I think I might be able to help out."

Roe looked up with the cigarette hanging in his lips. "Just you? Selby said you had a kid workin' for you, looked like he might be a hand."

"I can't speak for him. He just did this one job for me, and now he's on his own."

Roe lit his cigarette. "Oh. I thought he was workin' for you."

"He was."

"Hmm." Roe flicked the match on the ground.

"Anyway, that was the main reason I dropped in. If I'd known you were at Selby's, I'd have stopped there."

"All the same." The pale brown eyes wandered across Fielding's two horses. Then Roe walked to the chair Isabel left out, and he sat down with a sigh. "Sit here in the shade," he said. He glanced at the stool. "You in a hurry?"

"Not really," said Fielding. "I picked up this horse in town, and I was takin' him back to my camp. And I've got things to do there."

"I imagine." Roe lifted the cigarette to his lips as he gazed off to the east.

Fielding waited for the man to say more, but he didn't. After a long moment, Fielding said, "Well, I guess I might be movin' along before it warms up any more."

"Oh, yeah," said Roe. "Thanks for stoppin'. I'll tell Bill I talked to you."

"That'll be fine. What do you think, in about a week?"

"Somethin' like that. We'll let you know ahead of time. And if you can get that kid to go, we could use him, too."

Fielding saw a bit of humor in Roe acting like a roundup boss, but he just said, "I'll mention it if I talk to him."

"Do that." Roe gave a backhand swipe at the goat, which had drawn near.

"Well, so long, then," said Fielding.

"Sure. We'll see you later."

Fielding turned the two horses and led them away. When he stopped to get them into position, he looked toward the stable. He expected to see Isabel, and there she was. She had unsaddled her papa's horse and was leading him out into the sunlight. Fielding waved, and Isabel waved back. Then he stepped up into the saddle, nudged the buckskin, and set out with the brown horse at his side.

CHAPTER THREE

The song of the lark fluted in the morning air as Fielding drank his coffee. Seated on a pile of canvas and using one of the two log sections for a workbench, he devoted his attention to putting a D-ring on a lash cinch. With his smallest punch he had made two sets of matching holes in the leather. Now, with the ring in place and the strap folded over, he was doing the stitching with two strands of waxed thread, each pulled with a two-inch needle. After a whole winter in which to go through his gear and make repairs, it took but one trip to bring this detail to his attention. The rope knot was about to pull through the eye of the leather, and putting on a D-ring now would save a lot of trouble later. Fielding was glad to have the time, and the peace and quiet, to tend to it.

When he was done with his work and had his equipment put away, he saddled the dark horse he had kept in the corral overnight. Shading in color from deepest brown to black, the horse was well built for packing, with close quarters and a thick body. He was also a good saddle horse, poky at times, and Fielding had to ride him every once in a while to keep him in tune.

With the horse rigged and ready to go, Fielding went out to gather the loose stock and bring them, with the picket horses, into the corral for the day. He looked over each one as he took the bells off, and finding no cuts or scratches, he climbed through the poles and put the bells and picket ropes in the gear tent. Then he led the dark horse out a few steps and mounted up.

He rode south through the grassland, following the course of Antelope Creek but staying up and away from the cutbanks and debris. Lodge's place was about four miles off, and the first half of the way had easier riding on this side of the creek. Fielding relaxed in the saddle and gazed at the rangeland as it rolled out to the southwest.

The dark horse seemed restless, however. He was throwing his head and snorting, so Fielding put him on a lope for half a mile. When they slowed to a walk again, the horse settled down.

Fielding rode on until the little valley narrowed. He reined the horse to the left, went down a short bank, and crossed the creek in a wide, shallow spot where he could see pebbles in the silt below. The creek was less than a foot deep here, so the dark horse splashed right through and climbed up on the opposite bank. Fielding pointed the horse south again, with the creek now on his right.

A quarter of a mile later, Fielding thought he saw movement through the trees where the watercourse made a bend in front of him. Riding out and around and then veering to his right, he came upon a camp. Foremost in the site and a little to the left stood a small box elder tree about ten feet tall with a curved trunk and full foliage. In the background, a grove of young cottonwoods rose to a height of twenty feet or so. Midway between the box elder and the cottonwoods sat a pyramid-shaped tepee tent, and to the right edge of the site a blackish mule stood tied to one of the cottonwoods. A human form stepped into view from behind the mule and called out.

"What do you want?" The voice came in a growl.

Fielding reined his horse to a stop and took a full look at the man. He was a dark, wild-looking character, topped with a battered, full-crowned hat with a flat brim. Long hair flowed out on the sides and matched the spreading beard in its unruly appearance. The man was not armed, so Fielding did not sense a great deal to fear. He knew that some men, especially prospectors but other loners as well, were jealous about their campsites, so he dismounted and held his reins. If the man was camped in this area, it was worthwhile to know what he was up to.

"Mornin'," said Fielding.

"What do you want?" came the voice again.

"Nothin' in particular. I saw your camp, so I thought I'd stop and say hello."

"Well, hallo, then."

Fielding walked forward with the horse tagging along. The wild-looking man took a few steps forward as well, and when Fielding was within five yards he stopped and smiled at the man. "Name's Tom Fielding," he said. "I've got a camp myself, about two miles downstream on the other side."

"Cattleman?"

"No, I'm a packer."

The man's eyes widened, and Fielding saw that they were of that changeable color called hazel. "I don't like these sons a' bitches that think they can run cattle through your camp. Think they own the whole range, but they don't. This is public."

"I know."

"For every dollar they make, a poor man's sweated some of his life away. They walk on the backs of the workin'man. Rich as Kreesus, with more than they ever need."

Fielding shrugged. "Some of these cattlemen don't have much."

The hazel eyes flashed. "I'm talkin' about them that does. Hand in glove with the robber barons, Morgan and Stanford and the rest. For every railroad tie they laid, a laboring-man died. Everyone knows it, but the rich just get richer and keep the poor man under his heel." As the man spoke, his yellow teeth showed, and flecks of saliva flew out.

"I don't doubt it," said Fielding. At first he was surprised at how the man launched into his diatribe, but he was beginning to place the fellow now. Mahoney had said there was a crazy man living out this way. So he had been here over a week at least.

"Everywhere you go," continued the stranger. "Railroads, cattle barons, slaughterhouses, gold and silver mines. They send men down into hard-rock mines to die in the poison air like canaries. And they wonder why people blow 'em up!"

59

Fielding winced. That kind of talk made him uneasy. Keeping his voice calm, he said, "This is not a bad place to be. We leave one another alone, at least I do, and so does our good neighbor Lodge, off to the south here. Couldn't ask for better."

"Oh, *he's* all right."

"Sure he is. And I'm no robber baron myself. If you ever need anything, don't be afraid to ask. If I'm around, I'll help. That is, if it's within my means."

"I don't go visitin' much."

"That's all right, too. By the way, friend, if it's not too forward of me to ask, what do you go by?"

The stranger had a matter-of-fact expression on his face, as if he were buying a sack of flour. "My name? It's Dunvil."

"Good enough, friend." Fielding held out his hand.

Dunvil shook. He was an average-sized man, and he had a normal handshake.

Fielding stepped back with his horse. "Well, I think I'll be on my way," he said. "I'll see you later."

"If I'm here."

Fielding paused at the crest of a hill and looked downslope at Lodge's homestead. At each corner of the one-hundred-and-sixty-acre parcel, a pile of rocks marked the boundary of what Lodge called the Magpie. It was a hardscrabble place, with sparse grass competing with prickly pear and sagebrush, but Lodge had a neat, clean layout. The house, a two-room cabin made of lumber already weathered, faced south. To the west of it stood an equally grayed stable and a plank corral. Lodge himself was standing in the middle of his property with his two sorrels, so Fielding rode down to meet him.

The horses looked up, and one of them nickered. Lodge turned and waved.

As Fielding came to a stop and dismounted, he saw that the two horses were loose and Lodge did not have a rope or halter with him. To all appearances, he had been having a conversation with the sorrels. They were well matched, each with white socks on the hind legs, and one with a blaze narrower than the other's.

"How do you do?" said Fielding.

"Came to see me in your time of leisure, did you?"

"Looks like it. Did I interrupt a conversation?"

"Nothing that can't wait." Lodge bent over, picked up a reddish pink stone a little smaller than a hen's egg, and put it in his trouser pocket. He eyed the dark horse and said, "If you want to, we can go up to the house, and you can give him some water."

"That's fine." Fielding turned and walked side by side with Lodge as the two sorrels followed.

"Grass is takin' a while to grow," said Lodge.

"It varies. It's pretty good in the valley."

"Oh, yeah. My few head don't wander that far, and if I didn't keep 'em back here closer, those gun-happy cowpunchers would run 'em off anyway."

"I imagine."

They walked the rest of the way up the slope without talking. At the cabin door, Lodge reached into his pocket and dropped a handful of stones, the reddish one among them, onto a small pile. A white stone and a dark one also settled into place. Without a word, Lodge walked to the trough in front of the stable and started pumping.

Lodge was about forty-five by Fielding's guess, but he was in good shape for his age. No exertion seemed to bother him. After walking up the hill and now working the pump, he was breathing easy. As the water splashed out, he said, "Go ahead."

Fielding took off his hat and set it on the saddle horn, then bent over and cupped his hands. After washing off his face, he caught water for a drink.

"That's good," he said. "Thanks."

The dark horse had put his lower lip below the surface of the water and was taking in a drink. Lodge pumped a few more times and let the handle rest.

"I'll put these two away," he said. He made a clicking sound with the corner of his mouth, and the pair of sorrels followed him to the corral gate. When he opened it, they walked in and turned around. He closed the gate and slid the board latch.

The dark horse lifted his dripping muzzle as Lodge came back.

"Do you want to tie him up?"

"I could," Fielding answered. He led the horse to the hitching rail and wrapped the reins. As he walked back toward the trough, Lodge spoke.

"What's new today?"

Fielding reflected. "I met your neighbor, or I guess he's mine, too. Said his name was Dunvil."

"Oh, him."

Fielding settled his hat on his head. "Seems like a powder keg."

"Might be. He rants like an anarchist. Did he talk about the kings who ride their carriages across the backs of the poor?"

"Not in those words, but along those lines. Says it all in a rush. Seems like he might be a long ways from those that think like him."

Lodge gave a shrug. "Like as not, he won't be around here very long." He laughed. "Unless he's layin' low from his last dynamite job. Here, let's sit in the shade."

The host led the way to a bench on the west side of the house. When the two men were seated, Lodge asked, "What else is new?"

"Well, let me see. Buchanan said he didn't want me to do any work for him."

"Huh. Because of your run-in with Cronin's boys?"

Fielding nodded. "That seems to be the reason."

"That figures. They stick together, you know, and Buchanan won't do anything to get him on Cronin's bad side. Wouldn't want to lose his support if he needed it."

"He doesn't seem that bad, otherwise."

"Nah, he's not," said Lodge. "He came here early and worked for what he's got. You can see it in him."

Fielding recalled the weathered features. "Oh, yeah."

"But he's got to keep his fences mended, so to speak. Too bad."

The trill of a songbird sounded, and

Fielding looked over to see a small black bird with white wing patches sitting on the edge of the horse trough.

"That's a pretty bird," said Lodge. "Lark bunting. Pretty song, too." After a couple of seconds he said, "Now, where were we?"

"Buchanan. I think we finished with him."

"Oh, uh-huh."

"So, after talkin' to him, I stopped in to see Roe. I told him I could probably help out on this roundup they're planning."

Lodge gave him an appraising look and said, "That's good."

"Work's work, and it'll be a while till some of these other jobs come in. And without Buchanan and Cronin, I'm going to have to scrape up a few more. But there's work. I'm not worried about that. It's just a little later."

"Sure. And you're young. You've got plenty of time to catch up. This trouble won't last long."

Fielding held his gaze on the older man. "You think it's trouble, then?"

"Maybe I shouldn't have put it so certain. I don't know how much trouble there'll be. Maybe part of it depends on the resistance."

"You mean, whether Selby lets 'em run all over him."

Lodge pursed his lips and nodded. "Him, and others. Like Roe, just to look close by.

But there's others farther out, and up on the flats, too."

"You think Cronin wants it all, then?"

As he took a slow look around, Lodge set his hat cockeyed for ventilation. Then he said, "Here's how I read it. The range and the whole cattle business in this part of the country has made a slow comeback since the big die-up of 'eighty-six, 'eighty-seven. But the numbers are up, and you told me yourself it looked like a good calf crop this year."

"From what I've seen."

"Well, we can figure on the basis of what we've seen and what we know close at hand. Selby's got about eighty head of cows, and most of them calved out. Roe's got half that much or more. Now, let's say there's half a dozen others on that same scale. Add it all up, and what's it come to?"

Fielding looked up at the underside of his hat brim. "Almost five hundred cows, plus calves."

"That's right. And from what I've heard, which may or may not be the straight truth, this fella that Dunvil would call a mucky-muck would like to bring in about that many more himself."

Fielding cocked his head. "Really?"

"That's just what I heard. Thinkin' to

bring 'em down from the Powder River Basin. One of his English investor friends has got that many to sell."

"That sounds like a big move for this bit of range."

"It does to me, too. But as long as the grass is free, a man could make himself a pile while the gittin's good."

"So in order to do that, he pushes out some of the small operators."

Lodge set his hat back on straight. "That's what it seems like. Push out one or two, make examples of 'em, and hope the others get the idea."

"It does make sense if you add it up," Fielding said. "He brings in a new foreman, and they go to work on someone who would be a good example."

"That was my tip-off. Like we said the other day, he's just a bit slick for your average foreman. And nobody knows him from around here. Chances are, he'll stick around long enough to do what he was brought in for, and then he'll be gone."

Fielding sorted out what he had just heard. "Seems to me like a big idea for someone."

"That doesn't mean he's a big thinker," said Lodge. "Most of these ideas have already been proven."

"I guess so."

"Especially the idea that a man can get away with what he wants if he's in a good position. You take the case of that woman they hung over on the Sweetwater. The ones that did it got off scot-free, and a couple of 'em ended up with some nice pieces of land to boot. That's no news. But you see, they had connections. Same with those over on Powder River, in Johnson County. They get a hired gun and a foreman both, and when they don't get everyone that way, they bring in a small army. Everyone knows that, too. The ones behind it had money and political influence, and they never had to answer for a bit of it." Lodge took a deep breath and settled down. "I'd better not get started on that. Makes me mad every time I think of it. But the point is, when the big operators pull stunts like that and get away with it, someone else figures he can do it, too. Bad part is, he probably can."

Fielding narrowed his eyes for a second. "You think Buchanan is thick with him?"

Lodge stroked his beard. "I don't think he's in on it, at least in the business aspect. But when it comes right down to it, these fellows stick together. Even when one of 'em doesn't believe in what the other's doin', he stands behind him, maybe a ways back, but it's part of the code. If you're in the club, you don't renege unless the other man has done somethin' that everyone can see is rotten. Otherwise, you can't count on someone else when you need it. Like we said a little while ago."

Now it was Fielding's turn to take a deep breath. "So you think Buchanan is hangin' back."

"I'd guess."

Two thoughts crossed in Fielding's mind. "Say," he began, "who's this snooty blond fellow I saw at Buchanan's yesterday? He came bouncin' in on a light-colored horse, no hat, all red in the face."

"Eyes that look like gooseberries?"

Fielding laughed. "That's him."

Lodge smiled, to appearances not displeased with his own humor. "The gentleman is named Cedric. I call him Cedric the Saxon, come to court the Lady Rowena."

Fielding's brows came together. "Who's that?"

"Oh, those are characters from Sir Walter Scott. Actually, he doesn't court her in the story. The resemblance is in name only. The young blade you met is one Cedric Tholes, as I've heard it."

"I didn't actually meet him. He snubbed me rather well, as they say."

"I can imagine. Anyway, he's British, which shouldn't surprise you, and he's stayin' at the Argyle. He's the son of one of Cronin's business associates. Plays polo when he's not among the uncivilized."

"Good for him. We won't miss him when he goes back." After a second, Fielding added, "I was wondering where he came from. Now it makes sense. She's probably the closest thing to his idea of class that he's going to find around here. Wonder what her father thinks of him."

"No tellin'. But Joe Buchanan's no fool." Lodge smiled as he wagged his head. "Just a mucky-muck."

"Well," said Fielding, "if there *is* any trouble, I hope Buchanan doesn't get caught up in it. I'd think less of him, and I'd feel sorry for her."

"Let him take care of himself. He's not going to waste any sympathy on you."

"Oh, no. He's shown that." Fielding's thought came back around to a point that had been skipped over earlier. "How about you?"

"How about me?" Lodge widened his eyes.

"What I mean is, how do you play into this bigger plan as you see it? Do you think they'll try to push you out, too?"

Lodge gave a backward wave. "I don't count for much. I've got twenty-three cows and seventeen calves, if I get 'em all branded. If they ran me out, they could use this place for a line camp, but there's better ones to be had before they get to me."

"That's good."

The deep brown eyes had a playful cast to them as Lodge said, "One of the many advantages of having so little."

Fielding glanced at the two sorrels in the corral. "You've got something, and you've worked for it," he said.

"Oh, yeah," Lodge answered, getting serious like before. "It's not much to someone else, but it is to me. I make light of it because it's mine, but I won't let someone walk all over me. I know what these sons of bitches are like, and I'll call 'em on it."

Fielding nodded in agreement.

Lodge went on. "That's the problem with Selby. I don't mean to say anything against him, but I think he might bend too easy. 'Course, maybe he knows how to stay out of trouble better than I do."

"He seemed to be stickin' up for himself the other day."

"That's true. We'll see how far it goes." Lodge stood up, moved out of the shade, and looked up at the sun. "It's early yet," he said.

Fielding rose from the bench. "I suppose you have work to do."

Lodge shook his head. "Not much at the moment. I was goin' down to bring in the horses when you showed up. I got that done." He squared his shoulders. "I was plannin' to take a little ride and check on my stock. I can probably still do that and not miss dinner."

"I should be going, too," said Fielding. "In spite of my leisure, I've got things to do as well." He glanced at Lodge and re-inforced his impression that the man looked solid.

"Come again when you can stay longer. I'll boil a spud and we can split it in two."

"Sounds good." Fielding unwrapped the reins from the hitching rail and led the horse out. He checked the cinch and mounted up, then touched the brim of his hat and rode away.

Halfway between Lodge's place and town, Fielding reined the dark horse to a stop. Ahead of him in the rolling waves of grass, two riders had gone out of sight behind a hill. This was the part of the range where most of Roe's and Selby's cattle grazed, but

Fielding did not think Roe and Selby were the ones he had seen. If the horse men were two of Cronin's hired hands, it would be a good thing to know.

Fielding dropped back behind the hill he had almost crested. If he kept to low ground and followed this line of hills north, he might come closer and get a better glimpse of the two riders. The dark horse had slowed down as the day had warmed up. Fielding gave him a nudge and got him to move out at a trot. The horse was rough at that gait, so Fielding put him into a lope for three-quarters of a mile until he found a broad rise of land on his right.

Twenty yards short of the top, he dismounted and led the horse up the slope. Once behind the prominence, he took off his hat and angled to the left, still moving uphill. As his eyesight cleared the low ridge, he first saw the rim and bluffs on the other side of the valley. He was facing northeast. He inched forward, and more of the valley came into view. After a couple of small steps more, he could see the next line of hills below.

As he waited, the vast rangeland was still and quiet. A faint ripple of air moved across the grass. Then he saw movement, color in the sea of pale green. A bay horse and a sorrel came out from behind a hill. The riders were closer than before, maybe a quarter of a mile off. They both looked straight ahead, and the horses moved at a fast walk.

Fielding recognized Henry Steelyard first, sitting straight up and easy on the bay. On the other side of Steelyard, the second rider showed above the haunches of the bay. Fielding recognized the hat with the turned-up brim, the reddish brown hair, and the black vest. It was the kid Mahoney.

From the distance, Fielding could not read the brands on the horses, but he could see they each carried one on the left hip. Some outfits branded horses on the front shoulder, but the hip was where the Argyle Ranch put its brand — one interlocking diamond above another. It looked as if Mahoney had found new work.

CHAPTER FOUR

Fielding saw the Argyle brand up close when he was in town a week later. A white horse and a dark one stood at the hitching rail in front of the general store, and each had the interlocking diamond pattern on its left hip. As Fielding had some purchases to make in the same store, he reined the sorrel to the next hitching rail to the left and swung down.

As he was tying the horse, two men came out of the store, boot heels sounding on the board sidewalk and spurs jingling. He saw at a glance that they were Pence and Adler.

Pence was dressed as usual, with his high-crowned dark hat, blue wool shirt with chest pockets, denim trousers, smooth-worn gun belt, and scuffed boots with spurs. In his left hand he carried two small white sacks of tobacco with yellow drawstrings — Bull Durham, from the looks of it. His face was clean-shaven except for his side whiskers, which grew an inch below his ear. From beneath the shade of his hat brim, his dull brown eyes looked out with a vacant expression.

Adler, as tall as Pence except for the peak of the hat, wore a white work shirt as before, and today Fielding noticed his gun belt. It was dark brown, blending in color with his low-crowned hat, clean wool vest, leather gloves, wool pants, and dark boots. Like Pence, he kept his right hand free and carried something in his left — rather than smoking materials, however, he held a stick of licorice.

As Fielding stepped onto the sidewalk, Pence gave him a blank stare while Adler nodded and recognized him by his last name. The two Argyle men paused at the edge of the sidewalk, and as Fielding walked behind them, he noticed that the dark horse carried a saddle gun in a leather scabbard. Once inside the store, Fielding glanced out the window to see Pence untying the white horse as Adler untied the dark one.

Fielding bought his supplies and took them out to his saddlebags. He put two cans of tomatoes and a pound of bacon in one side and two cans of peaches and a pound of beans in the other. With roundup a few days away, he didn't want to buy any more than necessary, so he hadn't spent much. As he untied the horse and led him from the rail, he pictured the inside of a café and a meal he would not have to cook for himself.

His thought was interrupted by the sight of a blonde head of hair and a full-length, pale blue dress. Susan Buchanan had moved out of the shade of an overhang and into the sunlight. As she was headed down the sidewalk in his direction, he turned and waited for her.

Her face showed recognition, but she did not waver. She walked on to the shade of the next canopy, where she stopped and said, "Hello, Tom."

"Good afternoon, Susan." He had the sense of standing in the street in the heat of the sun, looking up at the Lady Rowena, but he did not feel diminished.

Her voice had a courteous tone. "And how have you been since I saw you last?"

"Just fine."

"I suppose you've been busy."

"I've had to be. I've been out lining up new work. There's a couple of outfits I've packed for before, but I've had to get to know a couple more. It all takes time, half a day's ride here, a day's ride there. Get things in order, times and places."

"Oh, I'm sure." Her face did not move as she spoke.

"Of course, it'll be a little while till they take their cattle up to summer range."

"Oh, yes."

He hesitated, then asked, "And yourself?"

"About the same," she said. She held her hands together as she nodded and said again, "About the same."

"Glad to know you're all right," he said. "I'll let you go now." He lifted his hat and set it back down.

"Good-bye, Tom."

"Good-bye." As he turned to lead the horse, he saw her profile as she continued walking along the sidewalk.

Fielding mounted up and rode the three blocks to the café, which was located on the second street over from the railroad tracks. There he dismounted and tied his horse at the end of a row of others. There was no sidewalk here, just a worn path with fringes of grass, and he followed it to the door.

Inside, he looked around at the tables, which were mostly occupied, and he saw Richard Lodge seated across from a young man Fielding had not seen before. Lodge, who was not wearing his hat, raised his head and then waved for Fielding to come over.

As he made his way, Fielding saw a chair

on one of the two vacant sides of the table, so he headed towards it. Lodge took his hat from the seat of the chair, put it on his head, and motioned for Fielding to sit down. As Fielding scooted the chair under himself, Lodge made introductions.

"Tom, this is Ed. Did I get your last name?"

"Bracken," said the young fellow.

"Ed Bracken, then. Ed, meet Tom Fielding."

They shook hands, and Fielding settled into his seat. He noticed that the other two were both having beef stew.

"Ed's lookin' for work," said Lodge.

"Oh." Fielding looked at the young man, and beneath the dusty black hat with its round crown and wide, curling brim, he saw a kid of about eighteen. Bracken had short dark hair, eyebrows to match, and a light growth of mustache and beard. His brown eyes did not look up, and he had an air about him as if he had come in the back door and had asked to work for his meal.

The waitress appeared at the corner of the table, on Lodge's right and Fielding's left. "One for you, too?" she asked.

Fielding saw again the two bowls of stew. "Sure," he said.

"Comin' up."

As she turned, Lodge spoke. "Leonora, this goes with the other two."

"Sure," she said in a pleasant tone, and she walked away.

Fielding recalled having seen her before, but he had not taken notice of her until now. In Lodge's presence he saw her as more than just a biscuits-hooter. She was about forty years old, with a well-kept figure. Her brown hair was tied in back, and it swayed with the rest of her as she walked to the kitchen.

A minute later, she set down a large bowl of stew along with a spoon. Lodge glanced up at her without speaking, and she seemed poised for a second before she turned and left.

"Thanks, Richard," said Fielding as he took up his spoon.

"Pleasure's mine."

"Thanks again," said the kid.

"Don't mention it. And we're not done yet." Lodge gave the kid a friendly nod.

Fielding had to blow several times on the first spoonful, so he decided to let his stew cool down. He looked at the kid and asked, "What kind of work do you do?"

The kid's eyes came around. "Oh, whatever I can find."

"You work around horses?"

"I've done a little."

"Where did you work last?"

The kid's eyes went back to his food, and he gave a light shrug. "It was in Julesburg. Last year. I unloaded rail cars and loaded wagons."

Fielding noticed the kid's pale complexion and put it together with his wounded look and what he had just said. It looked as if this kid had been in jail, and his hair was just starting to grow out.

"There's work," said Fielding, "if you can keep from fallin' off a horse."

The kid turned and smiled, showing a set of filmy, uneven teeth. "If I do, I'll climb right back on."

"That's the thing to do." Fielding spooned a chunk of meat from the top of the bowlful. It was still hot.

"That's right," said Lodge. "Do your work and not complain, and you'll do just fine. You don't look like a complainer to me."

"I don't think I am." The kid's bowl was clean, and he set down his spoon.

"Here's the deal," said Fielding. "I think I can get you on with a couple of fellas we know. Small roundup, not much." He pointed side to side. "Lodge and I are both goin' along, and they can use another hand."

"Do I have to ride wild horses?"

81

"Not with this bunch, I don't think. Just a lot of dust and flies."

"That don't bother me."

"I hope not. And if you work out all right at that, I've got some work comin' up. Packin' supplies to cow and sheep camps."

"With mules?"

"I use horses. Nothin' against mules. I just don't care for 'em."

"I could try that, too."

"Eat your grub," said Lodge. "We're ready for pie, just waitin' on you."

As Fielding ate his stew, the waitress came and picked up the two empty bowls.

Lodge's brown eyes sparkled as he spoke to her in a gallant tone. "Leonora, my dear, have the sheepherders and cowpunchers cleaned you out of all your pie today?"

"Not at all. I've got one I made this morning, with only one slice taken out." She had transferred the bowls to her right hand and stood with her left hand on her hip.

"Apple, I hope."

"That's right," she said. She did not sound impatient at all.

"I think we'd like three slices, then."

"With coffee?"

Lodge gave a questioning look at Bracken, who nodded. "Three cups," said Lodge.

Leonora tipped her head toward Fielding.

"Did he say he wanted coffee?"

Lodge raised his lively eyes to meet hers. "He's my nephew. I speak for him."

Leonora gave Fielding a dubious look and walked away.

Out on the street, when Fielding saw that Bracken wasn't carrying a bag or anything, he asked the kid if he'd like to go pick up a few things he would need for work.

"I don't know," said Bracken. "I haven't got hardly any money."

"I'll stake you," said Fielding. "If you don't make enough on this cattle work, we can carry it over when you work for me."

"That's a ways off, isn't it?"

"A ways, maybe. But you'll need at least a pair of riding boots and a change of clothes. I can fix you up with a bedroll out of my gear."

Fielding looked the kid over. He was a tallish young fellow, not filled out yet. He was wearing a drab cotton work shirt, wrinkled and too short in the sleeves, as if it had belonged to someone else at one time. His brown canvas pants were holding up but needed a wash, and his scuffed clodhopper boots were breaking out at the toes.

The kid didn't say anything, so Fielding spoke again. "Come on, don't feel bad about it. We'll get you fitted out." He turned to Lodge, who stood by with reins in hand. "Thanks again for dinner," he said.

"Glad to." Lodge turned on his heel. "I'll see you fellas later."

Fielding untied his horse, and Bracken fell in alongside as Fielding and the sorrel walked toward the main street.

"Is he really your uncle?" asked the kid.

"No, he's just a good man. Knows a lot, too." Fielding recalled the shine in Lodge's eyes as the older man exchanged pleasantries with Leonora. "I'm beginning to get an idea, though, of where he gets some of his information."

The kid seemed determined to make a good impression. After Fielding had bought the clothes and a little more grub, Bracken insisted on walking the four miles to camp rather than have Fielding saddle a horse and come back to pick him up on the road.

"I'll get there just as soon," he said, "and it'll be less work for you."

Fielding relented and rode out of town. Once at his camp, he put the horses out as usual, then stored the provisions and rummaged around for bedding. He set out two blankets and a piece of canvas to serve as a ground sheet and cover. He put the parcel of clothes on top of that, along with a cotton sack for a duffel bag.

The kid came walking in a little while later. He had wasted no time. "This looks all right," he said. "Tents and everything."

"When we're on the trail, we don't usually set up this larger tent. That gear tent can be set up with just a rope between two trees, and we sleep in a tepee tent. Right now, though, it's all the luxuries."

The kid looked around. "What can I do? Do we need firewood?"

"I believe we do. You'll have to go up the creek a ways. It's picked pretty clean around here."

"I can do that." The kid craned his neck. "How many horses have you got?"

"Nine."

"Oh. That's a lot."

"Until you need 'em. Then you'd be surprised how many you need to haul a little bit of stuff."

Bracken made three trips with firewood while Fielding started a fire, put on a pot of beans to boil, and cut up bacon rind. The beans would take a couple of hours, and he could work up some biscuits toward the end.

When the kid set down his third armload of wood, Fielding said, "That should be enough. We're not goin' to be here that long."

"Anything else I can do?"

"Here."

Fielding led the way into the main tent, where he handed Bracken the cotton sack. "Here's your war bag. Use it for your personals and your extra clothes." Fielding pointed at the parcel. "There's your new clothes. You might want to go down to the water, get cleaned up, and change into these. Then wash out the ones you're wearin' right now. We're more than an hour away from grub, so you've got plenty of time. Oh, and here's your bedroll, just so you'll know."

The kid hesitated. His eyes clouded up, and he had to look away and swallow before he could speak. Then he looked square at Fielding and said, "I sure appreciate you givin' me a start like this."

Fielding felt a tightening in his own throat. "Everyone deserves a break," he said. "You get a chance someday, you do the same for someone else."

The kid blinked, then nodded his head. "I sure as hell will."

Bracken was clear-eyed and attentive when Fielding showed him the morning routine of bringing in the horses and watering those that had been picketed and penned.

"Make friends with that brown horse," said Fielding. "We'll let you ride him today. He's a good one to start with."

While the kid hung around the pole corral, Fielding put the coffeepot on the coals and sliced some bacon. In a few minutes, the smell of frying pork was on the air. Fielding mixed up a batch of biscuits, and when the bacon was crisp he put the Dutch oven in place of the skillet. By then the aroma of the coffee had risen to mix with the smell of bacon and wood smoke.

When the first tin plate of biscuits came out of the oven, Fielding divided the bacon onto two plates, along with three biscuits each. Then he and his helper sat down to eat.

"Dig in," said Fielding, "but don't hurry. We'll have the second bunch of biscuits with our coffee, and then we'll saddle our horses."

The grub disappeared, as did the second plate of biscuits. The morning air was still fresh, but the sun had gotten the flies up and around. Fielding put a lid on the cooling skillet. "We can use that grease later," he said. "We'll rinse the plates and wipe 'em, cups, too, and get started."

The area around the corral was well worn, so small puffs of dust rose as Fielding led the brown horse out. He handed the lead rope to Bracken and went for a currycomb.

As he brushed the horse, he talked to the kid. "Watch the way I do things, and do 'em the same way and in the same order. Not everyone does it alike, and you may have already learned something different, but as long as they're my horses, just do it this way. Same thing when we rig 'em for packin'."

The kid nodded and paid attention.

Fielding curried the horse, combed the mane and tail, and put on the blankets and saddle. "You'll get to know your horses," he said. "This one blows up against the cinch, so we'll tighten him again before we mount up." He put on the bridle, coiled the neck rope, and tied it to the front left saddle string.

Next he brought out the bay horse and went through the same process. The kid held the reins of the brown horse and stood by watching.

"Notice that both these saddles are double-rigged," said Fielding. "Always buckle the back cinch second when you're puttin' the saddle on, and unbuckle it first when you take the saddle off. If you don't, and the saddle slips around under his belly, you've got a hell of a mess. Maybe he tries to kick at it and gets his foot caught, and then it's worse."

Bracken nodded. "How about the stirrups?"

"We'll adjust them for you."

When the two horses were ready to go, Fielding waited until the kid was up in the saddle. Fielding took a last look around the camp, then swung up and led the way out onto the trail.

On the way to Selby's, Fielding explained the setup. "This roundup's a small enterprise in comparison with others. We get things organized today, and we roll out tomorrow. We'll gather a few cattle each day, but we won't hold anyone else's. This fella Bill Selby is the roundup boss, for as much as it amounts to. You've got to have someone in that position, and he's got the most cattle as well as the wagon. We'll go right past Roe's and could have met there, but he doesn't go out of his way to invite people to his place."

"And you say Richard Lodge will be there?"

"That's right."

They turned into the lane of Selby's place a little over half an hour later. A light breeze rippled through the box elders and young cottonwoods as Bill Selby stood in his yard waiting. He was about the same age as Lodge, and although he had a sturdy build, he was starting to fill out above the waist and go swayback. As Fielding rode closer, he noticed the man's puffy lower eyelids and sun-reddened cheekbones, plus a day or two of stubble that accentuated his square jaws.

Selby had a broad smile as he nodded his head up and down. "Mornin'," he called out.

"Good mornin'," Fielding answered.

"The others should be here right along. Go ahead and tie up."

Fielding and Bracken dismounted, and the kid took both sets of reins. As he led the horses away, Selby said, "That's not the same kid, is it?"

"No, I think that other one got a job somewhere else."

"Huh." Selby turned to peer at the trees on the west side, and as he did, the leather gloves in his hip pocket waved like the tail feathers on a bantam rooster. "Andy ought to be here right away," he said. "He's not that far away, and he said he'd come early."

A couple of minutes later, Roe came in through the trees. He waved to Selby and Fielding, gave Bracken in his new clothes a looking-over, and eased down from the saddle.

Selby smiled at Fielding. "Well, that leaves Richard. We can go in, pour a cup of coffee, and get going if we want to." He started out for the house, with his gloves coming into view again.

Roe finished tying his horse and walked past the kid without speaking. Fielding had the impression that Roe practiced treating young men as if they were under suspicion of wanting to abduct his daughter. Fielding had sensed some rebuffing from the old scavenger in the past, and he imagined that Roe was more civil to him now for the same reason Selby overflowed with friendship. Fielding was on their side now.

As Selby stopped to greet Roe, Fielding came alongside and introduced them both to Ed Bracken. Roe's glance slid over him again, and Selby said, "You can watch the horses if you want. If an old boy comes in from thataway, you can tell him we're inside."

"He means Lodge," said Fielding.

Bracken's dusty hat went up and down as he nodded.

Selby led the way inside to the kitchen, where four wooden chairs sat around a table covered with a stained oilcloth. To the right stood a grease-spattered cookstove, and to the left a stack of dirty dishes sat on the sideboard.

"Have a seat," said the host, looking out the window. "Hey, here's Richard now." He set out four cups, lifted a blue enamel coffeepot from the stove, and poured out the coffee.

Lodge knocked as he opened the door, and Selby called for him to come in. Greetings went around as Lodge came into the kitchen.

When everyone was seated, Selby began. "Here's how I've got it figured. If anyone else has a different idea, why, let me know." His light blue eyes moved around the table, and he continued. "I've got the wagon, as you know. Along with that I've got ten or twelve horses — at least ten that'll work. The other two are pretty green until I get someone to ride 'em. Richard, you've got two, and, Andy, you've got half a dozen, you said."

Roe's eyes opened and closed. "That's right. I need to leave one at home, just in case."

"That's fine. Now, let's see. How many more do we have?" The blue eyes came to Fielding.

"I've got nine head. I think most of 'em

92

will do all right. A couple of the slow, steady ones might do best at night herding."

"Or wagon horses."

Fielding did not answer.

Selby went on. "Of course, a couple of mine can do that. Bring all of yours along, though, so you can at least keep track of 'em."

Lodge spoke up. "Did you get anyone else?"

"I've got a wheat farmer named Mullins and his twelve-year-old kid lined up to do the cookin' and wranglin'. Him and his brother farm together, and they take turns hirin' out. They don't want to take any horses off the farm if they don't have to, though. They don't have many to begin with, as far as that's concerned, and they're probably all plugs and nags anyway."

After a couple of seconds, Lodge said, "That gives us a little more than twenty-five head."

"We should be all right," said Selby. "We're not goin' to be ridin' long and hard every day." He looked around the table again. "Mullins and his kid are comin' down this afternoon. I've got all the grub, and they'll double-bag it and load it in the wagon." He paused. "What else? Tom, what do you think of a tent?"

Fielding had raised his coffee cup and now set it down. "I've got a couple. I think the bigger one would be good for a mess tent or other general purposes, even sleeping. Do you have poles?" He pictured a typical chuck wagon with a couple of long poles tied alongside.

"No, I don't. Can't we use yours?"

"They're kind of long to pack down here on horses. I could drag 'em, but that might not be good. I usually just leave 'em put, and use 'em the next time I'm there. Make new ones if I go to a place I haven't been. But I don't think we'll see many lodgepole pines where we're goin'."

Lodge spoke again. "Is it too much trouble to send a wagon up to his camp?"

Selby moved his head back and forth. "I guess I could. I didn't have that much time figured in for such a little thing."

"I don't see anything wrong with it," said Roe as he rubbed his face.

"Ah, hell. Go ahead. Richard, maybe you can take my buckboard up there. I've got to stay here for Mullins. It'll be worth it to have a good tent, though. Do you sleep in it, Tom?"

"I do now, but I'll bring along a tepee tent for me and the kid to sleep in. This big one will sleep half a dozen, though. That's why the poles are so long."

"You think that kid's all right?" asked Selby.

"I think so. He catches on pretty quick."

"He looks like he eats a lot," said Roe.

"They all do," Lodge said. "We'll be glad to have him along."

Fielding spoke again. "One other small thing. I was hopin' to find a place to store the gear I won't be using. Packsaddles, panniers, canvas, the gear tent."

Selby pushed out his lower lip. "We'll find a place in the barn."

"We can bring all that stuff in the wagon, too," said Lodge. "Save you the trouble of packin' 'em all up."

Selby laid his hands flat on the table. "That should be pretty good, then. You boys come back this afternoon or evenin', and we all roll out in the mornin'. This ought to be an easy job."

CHAPTER FIVE

The roundup camp came into view as Fielding pushed the cow and calf down the last draw toward the valley. Bracken the day herder, on Fielding's white horse with speckles and dark mane, was easy to pick out on the other side of the small herd. He waved to Fielding and worked his way around.

"Looks like dinner's ready," said Fielding.

"I think it is," said Bracken. "The others came in a little while ago."

"I'll go eat, then, and I'll come back and relieve you."

"Sounds good." Bracken reined the white horse around to watch the cow and calf that had just come in, and Fielding headed for the chuck wagon.

Selby, who knew the run of the valley better than the rest, had picked a good site for a camp. It lay about seven miles south of the town of Umber, on a stream called

Richeau Creek. The crew had stayed here one night and planned to stay another, taking advantage of water for the cattle and horses as well as deadfall for firewood.

Across the valley to the east, a lone formation stood out from the ocher-colored bluffs. It was of the same height and color, but time and the elements had separated it. If it had stood farther out by itself, it might have been called Courthouse Bluff or Courthouse Rock, as such formations were called in other places, but it had no name that Fielding knew of. Named or not, it served as a good landmark for someone coming into the valley from the hills to the west.

Fielding yawned as he rode toward the camp. One day had stretched into the next on this drive — warm weather, with an occasional afternoon shower but no hail or lightning so far. The crew picked up a few head of stock each day and branded every three or four days. Although each day cost money in wages and grub, Selby did not push the crew.

At the moment, he and Lodge and Roe were seated in the shade of the canvas fly that Mullins set up in front of the entrance to the tent. Out in the open between the tent and the wagon, faint wisps of smoke rose from the fire pit, where two Dutch ovens and a coffeepot hung from the iron rack that ran lengthwise above the bed of coals. Mullins himself stood at the tailboard of the wagon with his hands in a metal mixing bowl. At his side, around the far corner of the work area but not out of sight behind the chuck box, Mullins's son, Grant, stood with a clean lard can, pouring small splashes of water as his father commanded.

Fielding swung down from the bay horse, walked in for the last few steps, and tied the reins to the front wheel of the wagon. He glanced in the direction of the horse herd, where the granger kid named Topper, who had hired on at the last minute as day wrangler, seemed to be practicing the art of sleeping on his feet.

Fielding picked up a tin plate and a fork.

"You'll need a spoon," said Mullins. "Beans are in the first pot, biscuits are cookin' in the second one."

"Thanks," said Fielding as he nodded at the cook.

Mullins was a slender man with a thin, worried face, but he did his work well and without much comment. Unlike other cooks who acted as if they owned the chuck wagon and everything related to it, Mullins had the air of working in someone else's domain and using someone else's equipment. The kid was mindful in the same way.

The two of them had joined the crew with nothing more than one bedroll and one duffel bag between them. The father slept in the same tent as the other men and got up every morning between three and four. On nights when Fielding rode that shift watching the herd, he saw Mullins hang the lighted lantern from a pole on the end of the wagon. The kid, who was horse wrangler by night and cook's helper by day, slept when he could on his father's bed, or beneath the wagon, or in the shade of the tent.

As Fielding passed the kid on his way to the grub, he saw the heavy eyelids and tired face. He felt sympathy for the kid, who was likeable in his quiet way. He did not complain, and he worked alongside his father to make a go of things.

At the fire pit, Fielding picked up the wooden pothook, lifted the lid from the first Dutch oven, and set it on a length of firewood that lay close by. Steam wafted from the pot, carrying the promise of beef and beans together. Fielding took the spoon from the end of the rack and served himself a plateful.

The other men were finishing up as he sat

on the ground near them.

"Good grub today," said Selby.

Lodge set his plate aside. "It's all good. Just some of it's better."

"We're a long ways from the café," Selby countered.

"Oh, I meant this was a lot better than a good deal of the chuck wagon grub I've eaten. Boiled beans, without a pinch of salt."

"You must've ate with the Mexicans," said Roe. "That's the way they cook 'em."

"That's not who I was thinkin' of, though I've eaten with them, too. And even the boiled beans aren't bad." Lodge shook his head. "Better than boiled cabbage, refried the next day in old grease, or cornmeal mush with bacon grease mixed in. Sorry, Tom. Didn't mean to spoil your appetite."

"No danger there," said Fielding.

Roe took out the makin's and went about rolling a cigarette.

Selby picked at the drying grass next to him and said, "Well, this is slow goin', but we knew it was goin' to be that way."

"It's all right," said Lodge.

Roe spoke without looking up. "You got nothin' at home to be lookin' after."

"Everyone's got somethin'," said Lodge. "Well, almost everyone."

Mullins appeared with a tin plate of

biscuits. "Here, Tom," he said as he lowered it.

Fielding took two.

"Anyone else?" asked Mullins. When the other three shook their heads, he said, "I'll leave this at the wagon, Tom. Ed can have what you don't eat, and I'll make some more for the rest of us."

No one spoke for the next few minutes as Fielding ate his meal and Roe smoked his cigarette. Fielding went for a second helping and two more biscuits, and he had just gotten settled in the shade again when Lodge spoke.

"Looks like someone's comin'."

Fielding turned where he sat, and following Lodge's gaze, he peered to the northeast. Two riders were coming toward the camp. Fielding returned to his meal.

A few minutes later, the two men stopped their horses at the wagon and dismounted. They spoke to Mullins, handed their reins to the kid Grant, and came forward. Fielding recognized the man on the right as Joe Buchanan, while the one on the left took a few seconds to identify.

The man was of the same height as Buchanan. He wore tan canvas pants and a matching jacket, the latter open in front and not quite concealing a small gun and holster that rode high on his hip. He also wore a tan, high-crowned hat that sloped down in front. The wide brim shaded his features, and it was not until Fielding noticed the blond hair and searching eyes that he recognized Cedric the Saxon.

The two men walked in under the fly and stood in the shade. Cedric's gooseberry-colored eyes took in the men seated on the ground, and he arched his eyebrows as the corners of his mouth turned down. Buchanan smiled at nobody in particular. As usual, he was dressed in dark brown from his hat to his boots, and he wore dark spurs. Fielding glanced at Cedric's tan boots and saw a pair of silver spurs.

"Afternoon, boys," said Buchanan.

The four men on the ground returned the greeting.

"I hope your roundup's going all right," Buchanan continued.

"Slow but sure," Selby replied.

"That's good. We're movin' along, too." Buchanan took a breath and continued. "As you know, my outfit is in together with the Argyle's. We're runnin' a full crew, and right now we're on the other side of the valley and a little ways north."

He paused as the men on the ground nodded.

Cedric took the occasion to reach into his jacket and bring out a tan leather case. He pressed a brass button, and the case opened. He offered it to Buchanan, who took out a tailor-made cigarette, and then he lifted out one for himself. As Cedric put the case away, Buchanan produced a match and lit the two cigarettes. Cedric held his between the tips of his first two fingers as he blew away the smoke. Then, wrinkling his nose, he turned around to look at the rest of the camp.

Buchanan spoke again. "What I came to tell you is that we've made a pretty good gather so far." Cupping the cigarette as he held it between thumb and forefinger, he took a puff. "In amongst the stuff we've got is a few head of your stock." He nodded at Selby, Roe, and Lodge. "I believe we've got something of each of yours."

Fielding had the distinct feeling that Buchanan avoided looking at him. He told himself it didn't matter, as he didn't have any cattle. He went on eating his meal.

"If you'd like to come and get your stock," Buchanan went on, "sometime today or tomorrow would be a good time. We'll hold the herd, and you can cut out what's yours."

Selby spoke up. "I think tomorrow would work better for us. About this time of day?"

Buchanan nodded. "That should be fine. I'll let the others know, and we can be expectin' you." He took another drag on his cigarette and looked around. "This weather is all a man could ask for, isn't it?"

Selby smiled. "Couldn't be better."

"Well," said Buchanan, with an intake of breath as he drew himself up straight, "we'd best be gettin' back." He turned to Cedric, who met his glance and gave a curt nod.

"Be sure to get something to eat before you go," said Selby. "There's plenty."

Buchanan gave a short smile. "Thanks, but we ate before we came over."

"Good enough," said Selby. "We'll see you tomorrow."

"You bet." Buchanan and Cedric went out from under the canvas fly.

When the two men had mounted their horses and ridden away, Roe spoke up. "Who the hell is he?"

"Why, that's Joe Buchanan," Selby answered. "You know him."

"I mean the dandy with his nose in the air."

Selby cleared his throat. "I believe that's a personal friend of Cronin's. Isn't that right, Richard?"

"That's right. Name of Cedric. Sociable chap, as you can see."

Roe, who had smoked his own cigarette down to a pinch, said, "That's some kind of case he's got for his smokes."

"Goes along with his tin cup," said Lodge. "Did you see it tied to his saddle horn? He carries it so he doesn't have to get down on his belly to drink from a spring, or cup water in his hands from a stream. I heard he won't drink from the same dipper as the other men, either."

"Well, he's British," said Selby.

"What is he, some kind of a remittance man?" Roe's voice had a nasal whine to it.

Selby shrugged. "I don't know."

"What's that?" asked Fielding.

Selby looked at Lodge, who had leaned over to rest on his right forearm.

"A remittance man," said Lodge, "is a fellow, usually from England, who lives off his relatives back home. His family sends him money, in remittances as they call it, so he'll stay over here — in this country or Canada — and not come home and be an embarrassment to them. Usually some prodigal, I guess. But I don't think our friend Cedric is one of them. From what I heard, his father is one of your foreign investors in cattle. Pal of Cronin's."

"Well, I didn't like his looks." Roe poked his finger between his neck and bandanna

105

and rubbed back and forth.

Lodge gave a short laugh. "I doubt that he liked ours, either. But that's not goin' to keep me from enjoyin' a cup of coffee."

The four riders left camp after noon dinner the next day, leaving the other workers at their regular tasks — Bracken to keep in the cattle herd, Topper to watch the horse herd, and Mullins and Grant to clean up after the midday meal and start working on supper. Fielding wondered, as he did at times, at the efficiency of having four workers in camp and only four men to make the gather, but Selby seemed satisfied with the progress they were making.

The men rode two abreast, with Selby and Roe in front and Fielding with Lodge a few paces back. Unlike Roe, who slouched in the saddle and listed to one side or another, Selby rode straight up, with his chin lifted. He kept a cheerful air about him, which struck Fielding as being maintained for effect. Although Selby had shown resistance in the set-to with Cronin's men a couple of weeks earlier, he now seemed willing to go out of his way to get along with men from the other camp. Fielding had noticed also that Selby did not join in on the casual remarks about Cronin, Cedric, and the others. If he was hoping to avoid confrontation, he was giving it a good try.

The four riders made it to the other roundup camp in less than an hour. Fielding had seen it from a mile away, as it sat on high ground and had a thin cloud of dust hovering over it. Selby brought his horse to a stop at the edge of the camp, and the other three did likewise, as it was common courtesy to let the horses relieve themselves before going in as well as to stir up less dust.

At present, the Argyle and Buchanan crew was having dinner and taking noontime rest. Fielding counted fourteen punchers either sitting cross-legged or stretched out on the grass. To the left of them, under a canopy that came off the big tent, four men sat on folding chairs. Fielding identified them as Cronin, Cedric, Buchanan, and Adler. To the right, the chuck wagon cook and his helper moved between the fire pit and the tail end of the wagon. Farther back, to the right, an empty wagon that would serve as the bed wagon for hauling bedrolls between camps now stood as the base for the rope corral that held the horse herd. Fielding estimated over a hundred head in the bunch, plus the day wrangler's horse, tied to a wagon wheel, another horse tied to the chuck wagon, and four or five that were ground-hitched beyond the tent and canopy. Farther back yet, two day herders on horseback rode around the cattle herd, which looked as if it held from three to four hundred head. The mooing and bawling of the cattle rose in the constant din a man got used to on roundup grounds.

Fielding was thinking that he and Lodge could stand back and hold the horses, but Selby turned and said over his shoulder, "Don't lag behind, boys. Come right in behind me." So Fielding and Lodge followed the other two up to the edge of the shade, and Fielding moved to one side so he could see the men seated.

Closest to him, sitting upright with his hands on his knees, was J. P. Cronin. Fielding guessed him to be somewhere in his fifties, as he had blond hair running to silver, eyes bulging in a florid face, and a waistline spreading beneath his waistcoat. He was clean-shaven, and he showed a mouth full of teeth as he smiled. He wore a cream-colored hat, furrowed on top with a dent along each side, then a tan, frock-style coat with matching pants and vest, a gold watch chain, and an ivory-colored shirt with pearly buttons all the way down. His dark gun belt and dark-handled revolver matched his stovepipe boots, which rested flat on the ground and were trimmed with small silver spurs. Still smiling, Cronin rotated his head to take in the four visitors, and with his left hand he raised a dark cigar to his mouth.

He took a puff, and as the cloud drifted up, he said, "Hello, boys."

Cedric used the moment to take out his cigarette case, open it, and offer it to Buchanan and Adler. Buchanan accepted a cigarette, while Adler declined with a shake of the head. The foreman tugged on a watch chain, pulled out a silver watch, and began to wind it.

Selby answered, "Good afternoon, sir."

"Come for your stock, did you?"

"That's right, sir."

Cronin smiled as he rested his cigar hand on his knee. "I'm glad you did." His body heaved upward and then relaxed as he took a breath. "Here's how I think we can do it. We didn't separate your cattle because we didn't have a place to put them, so you can ride in and cut 'em out. A couple of our boys'll hold 'em for you, and when you're done you can each sign for what you got, and be on your way. Shouldn't take long, really."

Selby put on his smile. "Sounds good. We appreciate the trouble you're goin' to. We should have sent a rep, but we didn't have anyone to spare."

"It's quite all right," said Cronin. "As soon as you're done we're going to brand, so no one's going anywhere this afternoon anyway."

Fielding glanced at the punchers lounging around, and he noticed both Pence and Mahoney as well as Henry Steelyard and a handful of others he recognized.

"Real good," said Selby. He turned to the other three and said, "Let's go, boys."

They led their horses around the back of the tent, mounted up, and rode to the herd. Fielding was riding the sorrel, and he hoped the horse would do all right if he had to do any cutting.

The puncher who was riding the edge of the near side of the herd turned out to meet them. "I believe we've got thirteen cows, eleven calves, and seven steers," he said, "but you can see for yourselves."

Selby sent Fielding and Lodge to the far side of the herd while he and Roe worked the near side. The plan, as Fielding learned, was for one man to ride into the herd and cut out a cow and pass her off to his partner. If the calf didn't follow right away, the second fellow waited, and if the calf still didn't come out, he took the cow around to the men who were holding the cut. All these punchers of Buchanan's and Cronin's would have been keeping an eye on the other brands, and between them they would know which cows had calves and which didn't.

Lodge rode into the herd and brought out a red cow, and a calf came trailing a few yards behind. Fielding pushed the cow around the edge of the herd until he came to the day herder, who pointed to an area a couple of hundred yards to the south, where two men sat on horses. Fielding delivered the cow and calf, nodded, and loped back.

The herd was not packed tight, so Lodge moved in and among the animals without getting jammed very much. In a little while he emerged with a brindle cow right ahead of him.

"I think this one's by herself," he said. "She looks dry."

Fielding concurred and took the cow around.

Two hours passed, and little by little the men made their cut. They had all the animals they had expected to find except for one calf. The mother cow bellowed nonstop and kept trying to break out and go back to the main herd.

Selby nodded as he looked over the small herd and took a count. "Not a yearling heifer in the bunch," he said.

"If there was, they probably ate her and buried the hide," said Roe.

"No use worryin' about it." Selby pulled his gloves snug. "Let's ride over to the tent and sign for these, and maybe that last calf'll come out by the time we get back."

Fielding held the horses while the other three men went under the canopy. Cronin, Cedric, and Buchanan held the same seats as before, while Adler stood in the sunlight, his silver watch chain glinting as he turned in conversation with three of the men. A couple of other punchers stood by with saddled horses, while a couple more got their mounts ready for the afternoon's work. The rest, who would be wrestling the roped calves and holding them down for the hot iron, were standing in groups of two or three. Mahoney and Pence stood in the group closest to the canopy.

Selby and the other two small cattlemen took a while talking to Cronin and Buchanan, writing out their statements of receipt, and signing. On a couple of occasions, Selby's voice rose in an artificial note as he tossed back his head and laughed. Roe took out his jackknife and sharpened his stub of a pencil while Cedric watched. Lodge seemed to be keeping track of where

Adler mingled.

At last the voices took on a tone of finality, and Selby gave a closing laugh. He and Roe and Lodge turned away and headed toward Fielding and the horses. As they walked within five yards of Pence and Mahoney, the big man said something that Fielding didn't catch from where he stood. Selby shrugged and kept walking.

Mahoney's voice came out with a challenging ring. "He said something to you."

Selby stopped and turned halfway. Roe and Lodge stopped as well. "I heard him," Selby replied.

"He said he lost a sack of Deuce."

Selby's face colored. "That's no concern of mine. I don't smoke."

"He said he lost a sack of Deuce."

"Are you his parrot?"

"He thinks one of you might have picked it up."

Mahoney struck an antagonistic pose as he stood with his chin lifted and his thumbs in his gun belt. The sun shone full on his upturned brim and reddish hair, and his nostrils seemed to flare. His voice had a sneer in it, and Fielding thought he saw a method taking place. Mahoney would get the person riled, and Pence would take it from there. From the way the kid had gotten under Selby's skin, it looked as if Mahoney knew what he was good at.

"Well, we didn't."

"What did you put in your back pocket?"

"My gloves. I took 'em off to sign those papers." Selby reached back, pulled out his gloves, and reached up to give them a shake as he showed them. Before he could give them a second flick, Pence came out of nowhere with his right fist and punched Selby on the side of the face.

Selby fell back a step and a half, got his footing, and charged forward. Pence landed another punch, this one a haymaker that snapped Selby's head back, sent his hat flying, and knocked him to the ground. Before Selby could get up, Mahoney kicked him in the head.

Fielding dropped the reins and launched in. As he did, Lodge came into the scuffle as well, saying, "Hey, we'll have none of that."

Fielding got between Selby and Mahoney and gave the kid a shove. As the kid went backward, Lodge appeared at Fielding's right, to stand between the fallen Selby and the aggressor, Pence.

Mahoney came back with a wild swing, which Fielding batted away with his left hand. He was about to counter with his right when Pence shoved past Lodge and clobbered Fielding on the right temple. Fielding staggered back and got his eyes on Pence in time to see the big man come up with a roundhouse that rocked Lodge back on his heels. Fielding was getting his feet back under him and looking out for Mahoney when Cronin's voice blared.

"Stop it!"

Everyone settled back and held still. Roe had gotten well out of the way, as had all the punchers to Fielding's left and behind Mahoney. Cronin had his pistol drawn and had a clear line of fire on anyone he pleased. On the other side of the fray stood Adler, with his gun drawn as well.

His voice was cold and steady as he said, "Do what the boss says." As if for emphasis, his silver watch chain caught the sunlight.

Cronin spoke again. "Get that man up off the ground. For Christ's sake, you act like a bunch of hooligans."

Lodge glared. "It wasn't a fair fight to begin with. This pig hit him without any warning. Then it got dirty when this other one kicked him in the head, so you're damn right we jumped in." He bent over and helped Selby to his feet.

Adler's voice came up from the other side. "Just watch what you say, fella."

Lodge turned his anger at the foreman. "You're brave as hell, aren't you, when you've got a gun in your hand?" He faced Cronin and continued. "I'd think this was a setup, you hopin' that one of us would pull a gun."

Cronin's face fell, but before he could speak, Lodge continued. "But I know you'd rather do your dirty work in the dark. That's your kind of courage. Band together, and hire it out." He pointed to Adler. "And that's the kind of egg-sucker you bring in to get it done."

Cronin moistened his lips with his tongue. "That's more than enough, I think. Why don't you men get your cattle and go?" He put his gun in his holster.

Adler did the same and, nonchalant, said, "Everyone gets their blood up, there's no good comes of it. Let's just put this behind us and do our work. Fred, hand the man his hat."

Mahoney, with his face flushed, picked up Selby's hat and handed it to him without speaking.

"Thanks," muttered Selby. He put the hat on his head and turned to look for the reins of his horse.

Fielding tried to get a view of Buchanan, but the man had turned away. Fielding did, however, catch a glance at Cedric's long, expressionless face.

Selby found his reins, mounted up, and led the way to the small herd. The others followed.

The one remaining calf had shown up, so the four men closed around the herd and started it on the way.

Fielding, who was riding drag about ten yards away from Lodge, said, "It was decent of you to jump in, too. But I wonder if you went too far with what you said."

Lodge wiped at his nose with his gloved hand. "Oh, I'm sick of these sons of bitches, and I'm not going to lick their boots." Then he added, "It's a hell of a good thing no one pulled a gun, though."

Bracken, the granger kid named Topper, Mullins, and his son, Grant, were all at their work as usual when the men put their gathered stock in with the rest of the herd. No one spoke of the incident at the other camp, and Fielding hoped they could all put it behind them. But he remembered the man who had said it that way, and he had his doubts. It was more likely that Adler would just put it away until later.

CHAPTER SIX

The morning breeze soughed in the cottonwoods, rustling the leaves but not shutting
out the tinkle of the horse bells in the
meadow and the accompanying song of the
meadowlarks. The sun had not yet cleared
the young cottonwoods on the east side of
the creek, so Fielding enjoyed the freshness
of the morning.

The cast-iron skillet lay upside down on
the log, and the coffeepot sat next to the
embers of the fire. Specks of ash rose in the
low eddies of air that formed in the fire pit
as the haze passed over. Things were on a
small scale this morning, which suited
Fielding as he mended a shirt with a small
needle and thread.

Out from the camp, coming into sunlight
inch by inch as the sun rose, the clothing
that Fielding and Bracken had washed the
evening before lay spread out on clumps of
sagebrush. It had been limp and damp

before Bracken set out for town, but it would all be dry by the time he came back. Seeing that none of the garments had blown off, Fielding returned to his work. The change from sunlight to shade required him to blink his eyes and adjust, but within half a minute he had his focus and was back at it. As he pulled the needle to tighten his stitch, he entertained a thought about how he might spend a couple of hours. Bracken was not due back until mid afternoon, and no other camp work needed to be done at the moment, so Fielding had time to take a short ride.

The sounds of the Roe menagerie lifted and floated on the air as Fielding rode into the front yard. The two gray geese did not show, however, as Isabel herself appeared around the corner of the house and came forward. Her dark hair hung loose to her shoulders, and she wore a full-length, dark blue dress that was snug at the waist. Below the hem, her laced black shoes were visible.

"What a surprise," she said. "I didn't expect you."

"I didn't plan very far ahead. I had a little time free, so I thought I'd stop by. Are you too busy for a visit?"

"Not at all. Papa's not here. He went over

to Bill's, to get ready for the get-together this evening. But you're welcome to visit if you'd like." Her eyes had a soft shine, and her clean, even teeth showed as she smiled.

"More than happy to." Fielding swung down from the buckskin and took off his hat, again disguising the move by rubbing his sleeve across his brow. "How have you been?" he asked. "You look as if you've weathered all right."

She gave a demure half smile, then said, "I was here by myself, but Leonora Janken came out and stayed a couple of times. You know her."

"Oh, yes."

Her eyes moved in a casual glance past him. "Would you like to water your horse?"

"He can wait till we're ready to go. I'll just hold him."

"Why don't you tie him? You can come around back, and I'll show you something."

Fielding put on his hat, tied the buckskin to the hitching post, and followed Isabel. Past the back corner of the house, he found himself in the midst of more of her father's salvage. A rowboat-shaped galvanized bath-tub sat next to a wooden icebox with a sagging door. A rusty corn grinder stood cheek-by-jowl with a clothes wringer, the latter mounted on a small vat with vertical staves and iron hoops. Isabel led the way past these hulks to a wooden lean-to next to the back door of the house.

At the entrance to the lean-to sat a kitchen chair, and next to it squatted the three-legged stool with chipped paint. On the yellowed stool, a dark brown leather case lay open to display a row of narrow, shiny instruments. Isabel picked up the case, closed it, and handed it to Fielding. Then she pulled the stool away from the lean-to but still in the shade and said, "Here, sit down, and I'll show you."

She sat on the chair and reached forward into the storage area, where she pulled out a burlap sack that looked as if it was stuffed with rags. She set the sack against her knees and held her hand out for the instrument case. When he handed it to her, she opened it.

"See, these are my sack-sewing needles."

He could see them now, gleaming pieces of fine polished steel, ranging in length from three to five inches. The first three needles were straight all the way, like any normal needle but larger. The next two were straight also but flared out like a long spearhead and tapered back to a point at the tip. The last one in the row was flared as well but bent so that the last inch angled away from the shaft. Across the top of the row, two semicircular needles were hooked into folds of leather.

"These are nice," he said, surprised to see something so neat and clean in the midst of all the junk.

"Thank you. I thought you might appreciate them. Most of them can be used for carpet and canvas as well. The curved ones are more for upholstery."

He nodded. "And you sew sacks?"

"In the wheat harvest. It's just for a short while each year, but it gives me something for myself."

"I see. That's coming up before long, isn't it?"

"Yes, it is. So I get out my needles and twine, and I take a few turns for practice. I've got different stitches I can make, but I start with the easiest one."

She took out a four-inch straight needle, handed the case back to Fielding, pulled and cut a length of heavy cotton twine from a spindle on her left, and threaded the needle, leaving about six inches of loose twine coming out one side of the needle eye. Next she adjusted the sack of rags, twisted an ear on the right corner of the open end, wound three loops around the base, and pulled it tight with a half hitch. Then, after pulling another six inches of twine through the eye on the loose end, she held the seams with her left hand as she looped her stitches across the top of the sack. In less than a minute she had reached the other end, where she twisted the left ear and tied it off.

"That's pretty good," said Fielding. "It looks as if you could do one per minute."

"If they came that fast. I understand they do, with some of these steam threshers. They can keep two sack-sewers busy at once."

"There's not enough grain around here for someone to go to all the trouble of bringing in a steam engine, is there? That's what they tell me."

"Not yet," she said. "And I'm not in a hurry for it." Then, as if she caught herself, she added, "Not that I mind the work. I just wouldn't want to live for it." She motioned with her arm at the backyard. "It's like all of this. I can put up with it, but I don't want to live in the midst of it for the rest of my life."

Fielding took heart. "It's not in your blood, then. All this stuff."

"Not like Papa's. He can live in a run-down place cluttered with scraps, and it doesn't bother him. I can't say it bothers me greatly, not now, but I can't see it as the rest of my life, not any more than working for day wages on a threshing crew or in a factory. Don't you think?"

"Well, sure. It's how you yourself see it."

She seemed to be in thought as she stood up, took the sack by the two ears, and set it inside the lean-to. As she sat down she smiled at him and said, "And how about you? I would imagine you're satisfied with what you do because you chose it." She held out her hand for the case, and as he gave it to her, his fingers touched hers.

"Yes," he said. "I'd say I like my work well enough." He did not feel as if he had to be on his guard with what he said, so he went on. "I've never had much of anything, so I'm not disappointed with what I've got. I've never had a place of my own, and I think I'd like to do that. Have a place where the rest of the world leaves you alone when you want."

"That's a good way to put it." She turned her dark eyes on him and added, "Oh, I hope you don't think I'm ungrateful for what I've got. After all, Papa does have a place of his own, and I've never wanted for anything. I work because I want to."

"I understand that."

"And there's nothing wrong with that kind

of work. That's where we started, wasn't it? I said I just didn't want to live for the sake of working on a threshing crew."

"I don't blame you. Some of those machines make a lot of racket, especially the steam engines."

"Well, there's the racket, and then the drudgery." She paused. "And the people you work with."

"I've met some of them," said Fielding. "Here and there. Packed supplies for a couple of 'em a while back. And this fellow Mullins and his kid, Grant, they worked roundup with us."

"Oh, he's all right," said Isabel. "There are others, though. You don't know Ray Foote, do you?"

Fielding shook his head. "Don't believe I've heard the name till now. Did you say Foot?"

"*Foot* with an *e*," she said. Then, with an impatient huff, she went on. "He's the one thing I dread most about this work coming up. He's a sack jig."

"What's that?"

"Oh, that's the person who jigs or shakes the sack so it has a uniform weight — hundred and thirty-eight to hundred and forty pounds. He jigs it and passes it to me to sew. I can't stand the way he looms over me, always making eyes at me, showing off how strong he is, hefting the full sacks. But he's got the mind of a slug. And when he counts the sacks, if he has four rows of five each, he counts them one by one."

Fielding smiled. He didn't mind that kind of competition. "I guess that's the way work is," he said. "You can't always pick who you work with. But if it's only for a while —"

"Yes, but he's taken to Papa, making friends with him. Buys him a drink in town, gives him a bottle to take home. I think he might be at Bill's this evening. He got himself invited, and Bill said he could come down with Mr. Mullins."

"Oh, well," said Fielding with a playful smile, "as long as he doesn't keep you tied up all evenin', showin' you the muscle in his arm."

"Pooh," she said. "If you don't mind, you can keep me away from him. And don't leave before he does."

Fielding laughed. "I think I can do that much."

"I'm glad you're going to be there."

"I wouldn't miss it."

Her dark eyes met his again. "I hope you don't think I was saying anything unkind about Papa."

"Oh, no. Like I said, I understand. And if

some of this isn't in your blood —" He was about to say, "So much the better," but he left the sentence unfinished.

"He always says I take after Mama. You never met her, but she was a lovely lady."

"Oh, then I agree with your father."

A blush came to Isabel's tan complexion. "Well, I take after her in other ways. She liked music, painting. She was adventurous, coming up here with Papa. She wanted to see new places. He was young then, too, of course."

"Did they homestead this place?"

"No. Papa bought it from someone else who started here. Papa worked in a creamery in Cheyenne, and he met the man that way. He and Mama sold everything they had — except me — and came here. It wasn't good for Mama, though." She stopped, then forced a smile. "Let's not be sad. We were talking about the party tonight. You like music, don't you?"

"Oh, sure."

"Maybe there'll be music there. Sometimes Mr. Lodge plays a song or two."

"Really? I didn't know he did."

"Otherwise, it might be rather dull. Just Papa, Bill Selby, Mr. Mullins, Ray Foote —"

"And myself, of course, not to mention

you. I think the kid who works for me will come along as well."

"Oh, yes. You had better be there. If I get trapped into a long conversation with Ray Foote, I'll have you to blame."

"Fear not," he said. "I'll be there, if only for that reason."

Fielding and Bracken rode to Selby's together as the sun was slipping behind the hills to the west. The kid had bought a used Colt .45 with holster and gun belt, and he was fiddling with the outfit to see how it rode best when he was in the saddle. Fielding, who had thought the kid was going to buy a jacket for the trip into the mountains, found himself getting impatient with the fuss.

"I wouldn't be too worried about that thing right now," he said. "As soon as we get to Selby's, you're going to have to put it in your saddlebag anyway."

"I know. I'm just tryin' it out, to see how it fits."

They got to Selby's right at dusk and turned their horses into a corral. Two of Roe's horses, which Fielding knew well enough by now, were in the next corral, and one of Lodge's sorrels had a pen to itself.

Inside the house, Isabel and her father

were sitting in wooden chairs in the sitting room, while Lodge was in the kitchen tuning a mandolin. Fielding said good evening to all present, took off his hat, and turned to where father and daughter sat.

As he gave his hand to Isabel in fuller greeting, he was struck by her beauty. Although she looked fine to him in her everyday clothes, she was enchanting now. Her dark hair, clean and shiny, was held in place with a hair band that crossed her head a few inches back of her brow, and she wore a pair of garnet earrings. Her clean white blouse was set off by a black velvet vest and matching ankle-length skirt, with a pair of narrow black boots barely showing. As he met her eyes a second time, he caught a trace of perfume that made him forget where he was.

Her voice brought him back. "I'm glad you could make it."

"Oh, uh-huh." He widened his eyes and collected himself. "Say, I don't think you've met my wrangler, Ed Bracken. Ed, this is Miss Roe."

The kid had gone easy on his new clothes, wearing mostly his old ones during roundup, so his better set was clean but no longer stiff. He had followed Fielding's example and had taken off his hat, which he held in front of him as he nodded.

"Pleasure," he said.

"And a pleasure to meet you," she answered.

Roe sniffed and said, "Ed worked with us."

"Yes, I thought so." Isabel gave the young man a kind smile.

The expression on her face changed as more voices sounded at the open door. Fielding turned to see who else had come.

Selby was throwing his head back and giving his manufactured laugh. "Come on in, come on in," he said.

Across the threshold came a tall, husky young man with Mullins behind him.

Fielding nodded to Mullins and stood back so that the new arrivals could make a round of greetings. As he did, he made a quick study of the young man who made a beeline for Isabel.

Leaning forward at the waist and sporting a broad smile, the fellow took off his hat with a sweep. When he stood up, Fielding saw that he had a square-topped head, heavy cheekbones, and a long jawline tapering to a broad chin. He had a filmy complexion and light brown eyes that went with the tone of his dull, light-colored, coarse hair. As he put his hat back on, Fielding was impressed with how clean it was, and he imagined the man had taken it out of the box for this occasion.

Roe looked up from where he sat, and as he held out his hand he said, "Evenin', Ray."

The other man dwarfed Roe's hand with his own. "Same to you. Good to see you." Then he turned toward Fielding and said, "Ray Foote." With his elbow lifted, he brought around his large, thick hand.

Fielding met the impact and said, "Tom Fielding."

The light brown eyes carried a look of self-assurance as Foote released his grasp. "You're the horseman," he said, his voice a little louder than before. "I have a few myself."

"That's good."

Selby's voice came up from behind. "You shoulda been with us on roundup."

The smile came back. "Maybe next time I will." Then with a nod, Foote said, "Pleased to meet you," and moved on to introduce himself to Bracken.

"Likewise," said Fielding. He took measure of the man, who was more large-boned than broad-shouldered, though he filled out the starched, wheat-colored shirt that he wore. He was thick at the hips as well, and his tan corduroy pants covered the tops of a pair of heavy boots.

After Foote had made the rounds, he went outside and came back in with a narrow package wrapped in newspaper.

Roe sat up in his chair as Foote walked toward him.

"Thought you might like to open this," said the big man.

Roe took the item and peeled off the newspaper to reveal a quart of whiskey. "That's the good stuff," he said. Then he handed the bottle to Foote and said, "You can open it if you want." As Foote took out his pocketknife to trim the seal, the older man reached under his chair and brought up a tin cup.

Lodge, who had come out from the kitchen, said, "That's a handy cup you've got there. It's the same kind Cedric uses."

Roe cocked his eyebrow, and without taking his eye off the bottle he said, "You won't find me puttin' any water in this."

Foote poured a generous amount into the tin cup, then lifted the bottle as he turned to Lodge. "Care for a snort?"

"I'll have a little."

Fielding took advantage of the distraction to meet eyes with Isabel. She pointed to a chair nearby, so he crossed the room, drew the chair near her, and took a seat.

He looked up in time to see Bracken shaking his head at the offer of a drink as Foote held the bottle in front of the kid. Foote went on to pour a drink for Selby, and when he came around to Fielding, a look of displeasure crossed his face. He made a quick recovery of his smile, however, and said, "Have a drink?"

"I'll wait, thanks."

"Pour one for yourself," said Roe.

"I think I will."

Mullins, who had taken a chair by himself near the kitchen, sat with his arms folded and did not seem in the least as if he felt left out.

Selby, Foote, and Lodge remained standing. Selby kept the conversation going with the usual topics of the weather, how the grass was drying out, and how the crops were doing. He recalled years when the rain had never come, and years when the grasshoppers had been a plague.

"If it's not one thing it's another," he said. "You get good rain and no hoppers, and then you get hailed on."

"Isn't that the truth?" said Roe. He held out his cup toward Foote, who picked up the bottle from the floor where he had set it out of the way.

"I'm just glad that the roundup went so well," Selby continued.

"You got a good count on your cattle?" asked Foote, who seemed to adopt the knowing way of a cattleman as he squeaked the cork out of the bottle.

Roe held his cup forward. "Good as you could expect."

The talk subsided, and after a minute of silence, Selby spoke again. "Say, Richard, were you going to give us a song or two?"

Lodge swirled his glass, which he had not yet emptied. "I guess I could." He carried the glass to the kitchen and came back with his mandolin. "Any requests?" he asked.

"Do 'Lorena,' " said Selby. "I never get tired of it."

Lodge plucked at the strings, got set, and delivered the song with smiling melancholy. When he had finished and the applause died away, he asked, "Something else?"

Selby spoke again. "Oh, do 'Cowboy Jack' to go along with it."

Lodge's face lit up. "That's nice and sad and mournful. Let's give it a try." The mandolin made a thin, weepy sound as Lodge began to sing.

"He was just a lonely cowboy,
But his heart was kind and true;
He won the heart of a maiden
With eyes of heaven's own blue."

134

Fielding saw Bracken shift and look at his feet. The kid coughed, and Lodge sang on.

"They learned to love each other,
And named their wedding day;
But a quarrel came between them,
And Jack he rode away."

After another verse, Lodge came to the chorus:

"Your sweetheart waits for you, Jack,
Your sweetheart waits for you,
Out on the lonely prairie,
Where the skies are always blue."

Lodge sang the rest of the song, in which the cowboy comes back and learns that his girl has died, and the song ended with the chorus again. Bracken did not look up the whole time, but everyone else seemed to enjoy the morose ballad. When the applause was done, Foote spoke in his loud way.

"Does anyone want a drink? How about you, kid?"

Bracken held his head up, as if he was trying to keep from sniffling. "Yeah," he said. "I'll have one."

Selby fetched a glass, and Foote poured about three fingers. Lifting the bottle in

Fielding's direction, he said, "Are you about ready?"

"Not yet," said Fielding, shaking his head. "I'll wait a little longer."

"Suit yourself."

Fielding did not care for the man's tone, but he let the comment go.

Selby must have sensed an undercurrent as well. In his cheerful voice he said, "Give us another one, Richard. How about one of your own?"

Lodge held the shiny, blackish brown mandolin against his charcoal-colored vest. He had taken off his hat, and his dark, graying hair lay ridged and glossy. His brown eyes moved around the room to take in his audience, and he said, "Over half of you haven't heard me like this before, so I'm kinda shy, but I'll do one that Tom and Ed might like. I call it 'Old Rope Corral,' and it goes like this." He tucked the mandolin against him, sounded a few preliminary notes, and delivered the song with his full voice.

"As I sit on a log at the edge of the fire
And another day comes to a close,
Far away from the laughter and gloom of
    the city,
Far away from the laurel and rose,

136

"With the song of a stream as it chuckles
     in moonlight
Over secrets it never will tell,
I relax in the company of two faithful
     horses
Munching oats in the old rope corral.

"It's a mighty fine camp in the heart of the
     mountains
Where I come when my time is my own,
Where the shuffle of hooves and the wind
     in the treetops
Knock the edge off of being alone.

"As the fire burns down and the coals fall
     asunder,
There's a sight that I've come to know
     well —
A gash in the embers as bright as a
     blossom
Puts a glow on the old rope corral.

"Though I'm far from the plains and the
     tents of the wicked
And the company of my fellow man,
Just the warmth of the fire on the brim of
     my Stetson
Lets me think of the times in Cheyenne

"Where the love of a woman in cool

dusky twilight
Gave me hopes that I cannot retell
Of a place and a time far away from my
   refuge
In a camp by an old rope corral.

"For we opened our hearts and
   discovered each other
And made plans for the future as well;
But the rules of life changed as she
   pledged to another,
And the curtain of solitude fell.

"So I come to these mountains to stay
   with my horses
Where the water sings clear as a bell,
Where my tent stands in shadow in pale
   mountain moonlight
In my camp by the old rope corral.

"Well, the hope never dies that we'll find
   love again
Though the future we cannot foretell,
So we gather our strength as we take in
   the fire
Like the one by my old rope corral."

The room broke into applause, and Lodge
gave a bow of the head as he lowered the
mandolin.

"Thank you," he said. "It always makes me a little nervous to do one of my own, so I think I'll take a couple of minutes and find my drink. We might have some more later." He smiled and nodded to a chorus of thank-yous, then made his way to the kitchen. In another minute he was back with his drink.

The talk returned to the same topics as before — the weather, the flies, cattle and horses, and what the range was coming to. Foote, with no apparent sense of wordplay, declared that the homesteaders were getting more and more of a foothold. He said it as if he represented them as their leader and had a phalanx of foot soldiers behind him.

Lodge countered by saying that although that might be the case, the big cattlemen had an interest in keeping things the way they were. Then as a barb he added, "You know that, bein' a horseman yourself."

Foote gave a shrug. "Well, yeah, but there's plenty of land to go around."

"Say that when they come and cut your fence or club your sheep." Lodge took a sip of his whiskey.

"I don't have sheep."

"Neither do I. And you don't have to have sheep to know what I'm talking about. You can climb to the top of one of these buttes and it seems like you can see forever and no one's there. But they are, and even though there's a hell of a lot of land, it's not endless. Any range has its limits, and the more people you've got on it, the less there is for the ones who want it all."

It was evident that Foote wanted to hang on to his argument. "Well, some of it's deeded, so they can forget about it."

"That doesn't make 'em think they wouldn't like to get it. Especially if it's got a well or a water hole or anything they can use. You watch."

Foote's eyes, which had begun to droop off and on during the evening, opened wide. Before he could answer, Selby entered the discussion.

"Let's not get too worked up," he said. "I'm thinkin', or hopin', that things'll settle down as far as the neighbors go."

Roe with his drifting glance seemed to be looking at no one in particular as he said, "Oh, I think the trouble is over, or will be over before long."

Lodge wrinkled his nose. "Don't count your steers until they're in the rail car."

No one spoke for a few seconds. Mullins, who had said next to nothing all evening and had only moved his chair to avoid sitting behind Lodge during the performance, took notice of the talk about trouble. He rose from his chair and said it was time they started back.

Foote objected, saying the night was early yet, but Mullins insisted. The talk went back and forth a few times, and Mullins prevailed. With reluctance, Foote said good night to Roe and Isabel, nodded at Fielding and Bracken, and thanked Selby. Then he tugged down his black hat and walked out.

The room went quiet for a moment until Roe spoke. "I think you made him mad, Richard. He didn't say good-bye to you."

"Oh, that's all right. There was no point in gettin' worked up with someone like him anyway. Punkin roller in a Sunday hat." Lodge went into the kitchen and began to store the mandolin in its pasteboard case.

"Here, Ed," said Roe. "Why don't you hand me that bottle? No need to let it go to waste."

Bracken picked up the bottle by the tip of the neck and transferred it to Roe, who thanked him with a nod.

Fielding and Isabel turned toward each other. "It looks as if things are coming to a close," he said, hearing the echo of his words. "We've got a ride back, and so do you."

"It's not too far," she said, her dark eyes softening. "And we're in the wagon."

"Oh, let him go if he wants," said Roe as he finished pouring a drink. "We won't be far behind him."

Fielding met her eyes again. "I'll hitch the horses for you if you'd like."

"Oh, that would be nice. Papa won't have to get up so soon."

"Sure," said Roe. "Go ahead."

Fielding looked at Bracken, who had moved toward the door and looked ready to go. Fielding stood up, bid good evening to Roe and Lodge, and thanked Selby.

Isabel rose from her chair and said, "I'll hold the lantern for you."

"The kid can hold the lantern," said Roe.

"Then I'll show him where it is. I won't be a minute." Before her father could say anything, she was headed for the door.

Outside, Bracken walked ahead as Fielding and Isabel lingered in the yard.

"Thank you for staying," she said. "I was afraid he wasn't ever going to leave."

Fielding smiled. "We have Mullins to thank." He looked up at the sky. "Pretty moon, isn't it? Almost a full moon. Everyone should have a good ride home."

"Yes, it is pretty."

"Did you know you could see it with your eyes closed?"

"No, I didn't."

"Try it."

She closed her eyes, and he did the same. When they released from the kiss, she said, "You're right." Glancing at the door, she said, "I'd better go in."

"Thanks for helping me find the lantern," he said.

"I was glad to." Then she turned, and her black-and-white figure moved away in the moonlight.

CHAPTER SEVEN

Fielding hummed the tune of Lodge's song about the rope corral as he mixed up the batter for hotcakes. Bracken had not seemed to enjoy Lodge's songs, especially the second and third ones, but the kid was off by the gear tent loading and unloading his six-gun, so Fielding went through the plaintive melody time and again.

When the first cake was browned on both sides, he called to Bracken, "Come and get it."

The kid did not waste time. He came right over, picked up a plate, and held it out. Fielding lifted the hotcake onto it. "Thanks," said the kid.

"You bet. There's molasses."

Fielding served himself the second one and poured more batter into the hot skillet. After spreading on some molasses, he took a bite. "Not bad," he said. "Sometimes you wish for butter or honey, but as far as camp grub goes, it's pretty damn good."

"Sure is," said Bracken. His sadness from the night before seemed to have gone away, as he had a cheerful tone in his voice. "Say," he said, "what would you think if I practiced with my gun a little bit when we get things put away?"

"All right with me. Bein' Sunday, I didn't have any work planned. Just go down the creek a ways, so as not to make a lot of noise around camp."

They drank the coffee as they cleaned the plates, scrubbed the skillet, and wiped everything down. After Bracken rinsed out the coffeepot, he said, "I guess I'll go downstream for a while." With his hat on his head and his gun belt strapped on his waist, he wandered to the north, past some bushes and low trees, and out of sight.

A few minutes later, the bay horse in the corral gave a snuffle. From a ways off, footfalls sounded on the dry earth. Fielding held still and listened. The hooves were coming from upstream, the opposite direction from the way Bracken had gone. Fielding stood up and walked out to the edge of the camp, where he could see his horses grazing in the meadow to the south. A dark object caught his eye as a rider came around a low, spreading box elder tree.

It took him a couple of seconds to recognize the wild man Dunvil and his dark mule, as they had faded in memory. Now that Fielding had Dunvil placed, he could see that the man looked the same as before, with his long hair and beard flowing out beneath the battered, wide-brimmed, full-crowned hat. He wore a collarless, long-sleeved undershirt and a pair of flat-black suspenders. All three buttons on the shirt were done up, and the sweat stains and grime suggested that the shirt had not been washed or even taken off in a good while. The man's right hand was out of view, but his left, which held the reins, lifted in a small wave of greeting.

Fielding waved in return as the mule came forward. Fielding stepped to one side, as he preferred to give wide a berth to mules.

Dunvil stopped about ten feet away. It seemed as if he preferred to keep his own distance as well and didn't mind speaking in a loud voice to make up the difference. "You're back," he said.

"For a while."

"I came by a couple of times, but the place was empty."

Fielding smiled. "You could have moved in. Has all the comforts."

"Didn't need to. I've got 'em all where I

am." His eyes traveled and came back. "Except the corral. Don't need that."

Fielding cast a glance over the mule, which was standing still in a picture of obedience. Dunvil had it rigged with a heavy saddle with high swells and cantle, plus a large old iron mouth bit with a chain across the bottom and chains to connect the reins to the bit shanks. Fielding raised his eyes to meet Dunvil's, which were gray at the moment.

"I was workin' on roundup," said Fielding.

"That's what I heard."

"Oh, have you talked to Lodge?"

"I went to borrow some salt. For this thing." Dunvil pointed at his mule.

Fielding did not say anything, though he felt that the other man was waiting for him to speak.

After a long moment, Dunvil shifted in the saddle and said, "Heard you had a run-in."

"Not much. Just the consequences of gettin' very close to a couple of the Argyle men."

Dunvil spit to the off side of the mule. "They get a lot of nerve when they work for someone like that."

"I think they find each other. He looks for men like them."

"He's a high and mighty son of a bitch, isn't he? You got to see him in person, hey?"

"We had that pleasure."

Dunvil's eyes were lighting up. "I guess Lodge gave him what-for."

"He said a couple of words."

"I'm not that diplomatic."

Fielding shrugged. "I don't think Lodge is in danger of being called too polite. Not on that occasion."

"Well, it's a good thing I stay away from people, especially the likes of the Duke of Argyle. I wouldn't be nearly so nice."

"They're the type to stay away from, him and his men. I don't know if they're the type to put a hole in a man because of something he says, but I wouldn't want to push 'em far enough to find out."

"Oh, I don't go near 'em, and they'd best do the same with me. They come around and push me, and there'll be more than words."

Again Fielding did not say anything.

"I know their type," Dunvil went on. "They don't like nesters, grangers, or squatters. They want to have it all. Run cattle through your camp, ride in three or four strong, and tell a man to pull his stakes. All I've got to say is, they'd better not try it with me."

Fielding kept his silence. Some of Dunvil's talk sounded like a strange rehearsal of things the man had heard and said before.

"You think I'm crazy, but let me tell you this. The little men try to get together when the lords ride over the top of 'em, but it doesn't go very far. They either try to do it themselves, and some of 'em don't have the backbone, or everyone lays back and huddles like sheep and lets the Molly Maguire sons of bitches come in and run everything. Organizers. All they do is look out for themselves. You don't believe me."

"I don't know much about unions. They don't make it far in cow country."

"Not enough Swedes and Norwegians and other sheep, men that'll sign the oath and go back to muckin'." Dunvil's eyes were intense as he peered out from the shade of his hat. "If you want to get anywhere at all, I'll tell you how." The eyes narrowed. "You go for the top. Get the kingpin. Whether you blow 'im sky-high or cut 'im in half with a shotgun, you take care of the big auger. That gets results."

Fielding took a measured breath. "It's a way of lookin' at it," he said. "But I'm not likely to follow up on it."

The other man's eyes opened wide. "Oh, I didn't say you were. I was just sayin' what works, and why they'd better not come near me."

"I'd be surprised if they did," said Fielding.

"So would they."

Fielding could not gauge how much of Dunvil's rant was pure bluster and how much of it was vitriol of substance. Thinking that a change in topic wouldn't hurt, he said, "Well, I don't stay in this place very long anyway. Before too long I'll be off and gone on trips. Once these outfits take their cattle to summer range, I pack supplies up into the mountains to the line camps."

"You use horses."

"It works all right for me." Fielding observed the mule with its ears up and its eyes half closed. "This looks like a good animal you've got."

"Better than some. Slow at times."

Just to make conversation, Fielding asked, "Do you ever hire out?"

"What, to pack with him?"

"Oh, no. I meant yourself. Work."

"I work when I have to. Why?"

"No special reason. Just somethin' to talk about. But there is work comin' up around here. A little bit of grain to harvest, hay to cut and stack."

"That's all fine." Dunvil's eyes wandered

around the camp.

At that moment, a gunshot sounded from downstream.

Dunvil gave a suspicious look in the direction of the shot. "What was that?"

"Just my helper. He got himself a sidearm, and he went off to do some practicin' with it."

The gun went off again.

"I hope he knows which way to shoot," said the visitor.

"Oh, yeah. He knows where camp is. He just left here."

Dunvil nodded as he looked in that direction. "I didn't know you had anyone else around."

"It's a kid I hired to help me out. Gonna make a wrangler out of him, I guess."

Bracken's gun boomed again.

"Uh-huh." Dunvil raised his voice as he lifted his rein hand. "Well, I'll be goin' back." He squeezed the mule with his legs.

Fielding stood back as the man made a wide turn on the mule. "Good of you to drop by. We'll see you again."

"If neither of us breaks a neck," said Dunvil. "Hup, hup." The mule took off at a jiggling walk, showing the bottoms of its large, unshod hooves.

As the gun crashed again, Dunvil did not

look around. He left Fielding to wonder if this had been a version of a Sunday visit.

Fielding stood in the main street of town, where he had the two saddle horses and five packhorses tied to the hitching rails. Bracken came out of the store with two twenty-five-pound bags of flour.

"Right here," said Fielding, moving to the left side of the first packhorse. "We'll put one sack in each side. Keep the loads balanced. I always load the left side first, so these horses know what to expect." He took a bag of flour and slipped it into the pannier, then took the second bag and put in the right side while Bracken went in for more merchandise. After another trip, the gray horse had a hundred pounds of flour on him, which was enough for the time being. Fielding assumed he could fill in with smaller items in a little while.

He moved to the dun horse as Bracken came out with the next two bags of flour. After those and two more, the kid brought out rice in three twenty-pound bags.

A voice came from behind while Fielding had his back to the sidewalk and was putting the rice into the panniers on the dark horse. "Looks like we're in the same business today."

Fielding turned and saw Richard Lodge in the company of the woman Leonora. "How's that?" he asked.

"I came to help Leonora get a sack of four for the kitchen. So I'm her packhorse for the moment."

Fielding gave the lady a questioning look. "Is that right?"

Leonora, looking fresh in an off-white muslin dress and a wide-brimmed straw bonnet, gave a summery laugh. "That's what he says, but I can see that you're going about it in a much more serious way."

Bracken interrupted the conversation as he delivered three more bags of rice. Fielding put one on the dark horse and two on the sorrel.

Lodge spoke again. "Are you gettin' ready to pull out?"

"Almost," answered Fielding. "We'll take these goods back to camp and repack them. In the morning we'll pack our beds and camp outfit. I already left the big tent at Selby's."

"Then you'll get out on the trail tomorrow."

"That's the idea. We could have packed up the camp first, come down here, packed all this stuff once, and headed back west, but we wouldn't have gotten much farther than our own camp. Comes out about the same, and we don't have to haul the camp outfit down here and back."

Bracken came out with a full burlap sack on his shoulder.

"What's that?"

"Fifty pounds of beans."

"We'll put that in the next one." Fielding ducked under the lead rope and came up by the hitching rail, where Bracken handed him the sack of beans. Fielding cradled the weight and moved to the white horse.

"Good enough," said Lodge. "We'll leave you boys to your work, and we'll go on about ours."

"Have a good trip," sang out Leonora.

"Thanks," said Fielding. "We'll see you all when we get back."

Bracken continued hauling out supplies until all the flour, rice, beans, dried fruit, coffee, salt, sugar, molasses, bacon, and canned goods were distributed in the panniers.

"That's a lot of grub," said the kid as he came to a rest.

"It goes to two outfits. But we're not loaded yet."

"What next?"

"I need to get a bill of provisions for ourselves, which we'll put on the sorrel horse here, and then we'll put sixty pounds of whole oats on each of the other four."

Bracken's eyes widened.

"It'll be all right," said Fielding. "Some fellas put as much as two hundred pounds on a horse, but I don't like to put more than one seventy-five if I don't have to. None of these'll go over that, even with that bottle of castor oil I'm goin' to get for you."

The kid frowned. "What?"

Fielding patted him on the shoulder. "Don't worry. There's a bottle for one of the outfits, but we'll wrap it in half a dozen layers of newspaper, then roll it in burlap. It'll stay way out of reach."

With the camp provisions tied on top of the sorrel horse, Fielding stowed the loose ropes in the open panniers for the next step. He and Bracken led the seven horses down the street and over a block to the grain dealer's. Bracken tied the horses and Fielding went in to buy the oats.

Bracken carried the sacks out one by one, and Fielding centered each one on top of a load and tied it down. As he was finishing the fourth one, he became aware of someone watching him from the shade of an overhang next door. Fielding threw his last half hitch, stowed the slack, and looked across the hips of the gray horse. It took him a second to identify the man in the short-billed cap, dusty work clothes, and brogan shoes. The face looked wider than it did beneath the new black hat, but it had the same heavy-lidded eyes and dull complexion of Ray Foote.

Fielding ignored the man and moved to the front quarters of the horse, where he patted the gray on the neck and untied him. Leading the animal into the street, he said to Bracken, "Bring that dun horse around in back of this one."

Bracken did as he was told, and Fielding began the next task.

"Here's the way I do it," he began. "Even in easy country, I don't like to pull a string of more than seven by myself, though I've done it. When there's two of us and we use all seven pack animals, I take four and the other man takes three. Today, I take three and you take two. That'll be these two." He pulled a length of quarter-inch rope from the pannier, tied it to the dun's headstall, and tied the other end to a ring on the back of the gray horse's packsaddle. "See how I do it?" he went on. "You leave a little space between 'em, but you don't leave the rope long enough for this horse to put his front foot over it. Also, I use lightweight rope so that if they get into trouble, the rope gives."

The kid nodded.

"We'll go through this, time and again. Now you hold that front horse, and I'll get us another one." As Fielding turned away, he shot a glance at the shaded overhand and was glad to see that Foote had gone.

Bracken held the white horse as Fielding tied the dark horse on behind. "That sorrel does fine by himself," said Fielding. "Runs loose and tags along like a dog. Sometimes, like in fallen timber, you let all or most of 'em loose until the trail gets better, and you line 'em up again. Most of the time, though, you string 'em out. We'll let him go on his own today." He gave the horses a once-over and said, "That's good enough, I think. It's a short, easy ride to camp."

The sorrel trotted along behind and sometimes alongside. All the others moved in orderly fashion, raising a thin cloud of dust about stirrup high. The sun had reached the midday mark, and the air was still and dry as well as warm. Every few minutes, Fielding looked back to see how the kid was doing.

They followed the trail as it wound through the hills. When Fielding came to the lane that led into the Roe place, he stopped and signaled for Bracken to come ahead.

"You can get down and stretch your legs for a minute," he said. "Hold these horses. I'll be right back." He handed the kid the lead rope and turned the bay horse toward the yard.

The young nanny goat came out first to meet him as the cackling rose from the backyard. The front door opened, and Isabel stepped out onto the front step. She was wearing the dark gray dress and black shoes, and her hair hung loose at her shoulders. She smiled as she raised her hand in a wave, and then her gaze traveled past him.

"Looks like you're leaving," she said as he stopped the horse.

"On my way." He swung down from the saddle and held the reins. "I thought I should stop in and say good-bye for a little while."

She winced. "How long is that?"

"About ten days. We're taking these goods to camp, and we'll leave from there in the morning."

"That seems like quite a while."

He shrugged. "We don't get into the mountains until the second day, and we've got two outfits to deliver to. Comin' back empty, we go faster." With a wink he added, "Wouldn't want to waste any time."

Her face relaxed as she smiled again.

"Well, I'm glad you stopped in."

He held out his hand, and she came down from the doorstep and gave him hers. "Did you think I could leave without seeing you again?"

"I would hope not."

He gave a quick glance at the door. "I suppose your father's here."

"He just sat down to eat."

Fielding moved toward her, and they met in a quick kiss. As he drew back, he said, "Give him my best, then."

Her dark eyes roved across his face. "I'll be sure to."

He squeezed her hand and let it go. "Well, I'd best not linger." He motioned with his head toward the road. "They're waitin' for me."

"I won't keep you," she said. "That is, I won't make you tarry."

"I knew what you meant." He moved his hand along the reins in a preliminary motion for leaving.

Her face brightened. "Just a minute," she said. "I'll be back."

He watched her as she rushed into the house. A few seconds later she returned, carrying a small cloth sack.

"Here's something for you," she said.

"What is it?" He opened the sack, and seeing the dark contents, he said, "Jerky. Thanks a lot."

She stood with her hands together in front of her. "I hope you like it."

"I'm sure I will." Seeing no other pretext for staying, he said, "Well, I'm off. I'll see you again soon."

"Be careful, Tom."

"I sure will." He tucked the cloth sack into his saddlebag. He put his foot in the stirrup, grabbed the saddle horn, and paused. "Thanks again, Isabel. I'll be thinking of you." Then he swung aboard and rode away, looking back once to wave.

In camp, Fielding showed Bracken the process of double-bagging all the supplies and tying every parcel. He rolled the canned goods five at a time in a burlap sack and tied each one.

"Always have a few extra grain sacks," he said. "They come in handy for storin' rope, makin' hobbles, rubbin' down your horse. And you save all the strings as well, just as you saw Mullins do. Carry a few of them, and some leather lace, in your saddlebags."

After the supplies were wrapped, Fielding showed the kid the axe, with its head in a leather scabbard, and the shovel and the log saw, each in its canvas sheath. "You pack these on the front horse," he said. "You never know when you need them. Same with the hatchet and the shoein' outfit."

"What's the little sledgehammer for?"

"Drivin' picket stakes. There's another old saying for you — drive 'em deep, or walk."

"You don't have all yours staked out."

"I know which ones need it. And besides, this is home to these boys. It's not like up there." He pointed to the west, where a pink-and-orange sunset lit the sky between the dark skyline and a layer of hovering gray clouds.

The first hint of daylight was showing when Fielding gathered the horses and put them in the pole corral. Bracken in his hat and boots and old work clothes was feeding the fire.

After breakfast, Fielding began the routine of loading each horse. Starting with the gray horse, he reviewed how to put on the pad and crossbuck, tighten the britching, and cinch the rigging. Next he hung the panniers and loaded them, stressing as always the need to keep the weight even. The top pack he wrapped in canvas, then began a diamond hitch to tighten the whole load together.

"This is a one-man diamond," he said as

he twisted the two strands of rope on top. "A lot of this work goes easier if you've got two men, but you've got to know how to do it all by yourself." He pulled a loop of the loose strand up between the two he had twisted. "It's like cow-punchin' in a way, because at some point you're all on your own. You and your pal can play cards in the evenin' to see who wrangles the horses the next morning, or you can draw straws to see who rides the wild one. If you draw the short straw, maybe you snub the outlaw to your partner's saddle horn, but when the dally comes loose, you're on your own." With the second loop around the load on the other side, he pulled on it, and the diamond began to open up. "Now here's a rule for throwin' the diamond hitch: once you start, never give slack. See how it tightens in every direction as you pull this end. None of this is worth much, though, if you don't have your riggin' cinched good and tight to begin with."

He tied the gray horse to the corral and led out the speckled white horse. After that he loaded the dun, the dark horse, the roan, the bay, and the sorrel. Next he saddled the buckskin for himself, tying on the scabbard so that the rifle rode butt-up in front on the right side, where he could protect it from branches or pull it if he needed it. Meanwhile, Bracken saddled the brown horse.

Sunlight was coming in over the treetops as Fielding tied the horses three and three. With the sorrel he passed the lead rope up through the headstall and snugged it around the neck so the horse could travel on its own. Fielding took one last look around the camp, positioned his saddle horse and the lead rope to his string of three, and climbed aboard. Bracken mounted up as well, and the party moved out of camp.

The horses made good time, and the packs rode even. By early afternoon the group made it to Brush Creek, where Fielding decided to stop for a rest and water the horses.

"We've come over ten miles," he said. "Fifteen is all right, but in easy goin' like this I'd like to make a little more. We'll be goin' southwest after we cross here, and we can camp somewhere along Sybille Creek this evenin'. There's good grass all along there."

They found a good spot as he had hoped. They stripped the horses and watered them, picketed the dun and the gray, and turned out the rest except the roan. Fielding decided to keep it close for a night horse, and he gave Bracken another bit of instruction.

"Always tie your horse to a live tree, about four feet up like this. Don't give him more than a couple of feet of rope. Horses always pull backward when they get in a jam, and they don't know to let up. So don't put him where he'll pull a dead tree into his face or get a foot caught over the rope."

They went on to set up the gear tent, and they were just getting it pegged out when the roan horse nickered. A horseman was riding toward their camp.

As the man came closer, Fielding could see it was Henry Steelyard. The young man waved, came within twenty yards of camp, and dismounted. His round hat was set back on his head, with his wavy brown hair falling over his forehead, and he looked cheerful as always.

"Evenin', boys," he said. "Didn't know whose camp this was, but with that many horses, it figures."

"You're welcome to stay," said Fielding. "Private room, elegant dining."

Steelyard smiled. "Oh, that's all right. I was hopin' to make it a little further today. Just thought I'd stop and say hello."

"Goin' far?" Fielding did not want to seem inquisitive, but he saw gear on the back of the horse, and he thought Steelyard was a ways from home to be riding alone.

"I'm headed to Rock River. Know of a place out that way where I can get on."

"Oh. Did you —"

Steelyard's casual tone seemed deliberate as he said, "Yeah, I gave notice and rolled my blankets." He smiled as he looked up and around. "Thought I might see some different country."

"That's not all bad."

"I hope not." The young puncher's eyes took in the camp and came back to Fielding. "Well, Tom, I'd better be goin'. It's good to see you."

"Likewise, Henry. Good luck where you're goin."

"Thanks, Tom. You ever get out west of Rock River, don't be a stranger." Steelyard turned to his horse, poked his boot in the stirrup, and swung his leg up and over his bedroll and war bag. He waved to Bracken, touched his hat to Fielding, and rode off at a lope toward Sybille Canyon.

"Who's that?" asked Bracken.

"Oh, I guess you don't know him. His name's Henry Steelyard. He worked for J. P. Cronin for a couple of years, but it sounds like he drew his wages. Don't know why, in the middle of the season. He's a good-natured sort, minds his own business. Nice of him to stop in and say hello. You know, it seemed as if he wanted to let me know he was leavin' there."

"He didn't say why."

"Nah, and it's not the kind of thing you ask a fella."

Fielding and Bracken and the two sets of packhorses made good time the next day. They rode a full ten miles west through foothill country and watered the horses where a creek came out of a broad canyon. Higher up on both sides, pine and cedar trees grew among the rocks. Down below, most trees grew in the drainages, such as this one. Pale willows and dark cedars grew here, where the water flowed out of the canyon and rippled over smooth, speckled stones.

Bugs rose from the waterside plants as Fielding and Bracken walked upstream to drink the cool water and wash their faces. Fielding handed Bracken a stick of jerky and took a bite from his own.

"There's a place about five miles up where there's a set of pole corrals. It's worth our while to try to get that far today. Horses don't seem too tired, but it gets hotter in the canyon, especially in the late afternoon."

The kid nodded. His eyes had a faraway look, but he came back to the moment and said, "That sounds fine with me."

They finished the jerky, drank more water, and tied the packhorses together again. Fielding led the way as they went into the canyon.

When they got to the place Fielding had in mind, the corrals were no longer there. A couple of spikes in pine trees showed where poles had been nailed, and the ground was still roughed up from the last year's wear, but nothing of the corral itself remained except a few stubs in the fire pit.

Fielding let out a long, tired breath. "Isn't that something?" he said. "Someone took down the whole damn thing for firewood. Must have got stuck here in a cold spell."

"What'll we do, then?"

Fielding glanced around as he answered, "Well, we've got to make camp one way or another, and these horses need a rest. No reason to let them stand around with their packs on, so we'll unload everything and decide how to put 'em out. We'll have to cut some green stakes."

"And drive 'em deep."

"That's right."

They stripped the horses one by one and tied each horse to a tree where he was clear of the others.

"We need to set up the gear tent," said Fielding. "That's it there, and the rope is in the pack next to it."

As the kid went for the bundle of canvas, Fielding heard the sound of boot heels and spurs. Two men, who hadn't been on the trail a minute earlier, had appeared on foot at the western edge of the camp area. Fielding's stomach tightened as he recognized the upturned brim and reddish hair of one man and the high-crowned hat and dark side whiskers of the second. Mahoney and Pence had come to call.

"What do you need?" asked Fielding.

Bracken rose without picking up the canvas. "Who are they?" he asked.

"A couple of Cronin's men. Just stand by." When Mahoney and Pence did not answer his question, Fielding asked again, "What do you need?"

"Don't need anything," said Pence.

"Aren't you a ways off of your range?"

Pence wagged his head. "The Argyle runs cattle up here, too, you know. Or maybe you didn't know that."

Fielding shrugged. "What do you want here, then?"

Mahoney spoke up. "Who's that tramp you've got with you?"

Fielding felt a spark of anger jump inside. "What's it to you?"

"Maybe you don't know who he is."

"He's my wrangler. Or maybe you didn't know that."

Mahoney gave a short, sarcastic laugh. "You ought to know more about a fella before you hire him."

"I hired you."

"Not for long. But maybe you found your own kind here."

Fielding narrowed his eyebrows. "What's that supposed to mean?"

Mahoney lifted his chin and flared his nostrils. "Ask him."

Fielding turned his head halfway and could tell that Bracken was worked up. The kid was biting his lip and rubbing his left hand on his pants leg. Fielding came back to Mahoney and said, "You come a long ways to start trouble with someone who's doin' an honest piece of work."

"Listen to you." Mahoney sneered. "You don't even know what you've got."

"I don't need to."

Pence's gravelly voice came out. "Maybe you should tell him."

"He's a jailbird," said Mahoney, "in case you couldn't tell. Spent the winter in jail in Cheyenne. Tell him, kid."

"Go to hell," said Bracken.

"It was in the papers, so it's not anything made up." Mahoney's blue-green eyes moved sideways and back to Fielding. "Your wrangler here had him a little trollop down in Julesburg, but she ran off with a section hand. Didn't she, kid?"

"Shut your filthy mouth."

"I don't think you can make me." Mahoney's eyes moved back and forth as he spoke. "So your wrangler here followed her up to Cheyenne, and one night he gets liquored up, goes to their shack, and all but kills this section hand with a length of firewood. Didn't you, kid?"

Bracken was trembling and didn't say anything.

Mahoney went on in the same taunting tone. "And then when this jailbird was spending the winter in the coop, his little trollop has the other fella's baby. Didn't she, kid?"

"Ah, you son of a —" Bracken did not finish his sentence as he grabbed at his sixgun.

It must have been all Mahoney was waiting for. He pulled his gun and fired two shots at Bracken, which caused the kid to double over and drop his revolver. Then he pitched forward and fell on his right side.

As Mahoney put his pistol away, Pence raised his head in challenge. "How about you, packer?" called the big man. "Would you like to try it?"

Fielding's mouth was dry and his hand was shaking, but more than that, he could see how the whole thing had been set up. Mahoney and Pence, working together. Fielding swallowed hard and said, "I've got more sense than to be drawn in at this point."

Pence's voice came in short syllables. "Suit yourself."

Fielding turned away from the other two and walked a few steps to kneel by Bracken. All of the color had drained out of the kid's face.

His lips moved, and words came out. "I didn't even know him."

The realization came to Fielding that not only had Bracken not gone to the Argyle camp that day, but the others had not made much mention of the actual trouble after that. Chances were that the kid didn't have an idea that a feud had been in the making. Everyone else had, even Henry Steelyard. Maybe that was why Henry had gone to Rock River, and stopping in to tell Fielding about it was the most warning he would give. All of this came to Fielding in a couple of seconds.

"I'm sorry, kid," he said in a low voice.

He heard footsteps, and from the corner of his vision he saw the other two walking away. He put his hand beneath the kid's head, and the dark hat rolled aside.

"It's my fault," said Bracken.

"No, it's not. It's mine. I got you into this without thinking, and then I got pulled into the argument and didn't think straight enough to warn you."

"It's my fault. I got het up, and —" The kid didn't finish his sentence.

Fielding knew the kid had acted on his own impulses, but he didn't see it as the only source of blame. "No, Ed. It's not all your fault, and I'm sorry."

"Yes, it is," said Bracken. "All mine. She never did anything wrong."

Fielding could see the kid was going and he had things crossed up. Before Fielding could speak again, Bracken fell limp and was gone.

Fielding laid the head down and stayed kneeling for a long moment, with nine horses tied to trees and a kid who had died for the wrong reasons — a kid who had been grateful for getting a new start and now would never be able to give someone else a break.

CHAPTER EIGHT

Afternoon shadows were reaching into the street as Fielding stepped out of the deputy's office in Chugwater. It had been a ragged day and a half since he started down the mountain with Bracken's body, and the worst of it was over. It galled him to have to concede that Fred Mahoney had killed Ed Bracken in self-defense, but that was what it came to. The deputy had taken down the report and said he would look into it. He also had telegraphed Julesburg and had gotten an answer, so the body was going home. If there was one thing not to feel wretched about, it was the knowledge that the kid was going in his good clothes. They had been in his duffel bag at the time of the shooting.

Feeling empty and dragged out and edgy, Fielding stepped into the street where he had left the bay horse and the brown. As he checked the cinch on the bay, a voice came from behind him, saying his last name.

Chugwater was not his home, but it was close enough that he was not surprised to hear someone call his name in greeting.

Turning, he saw Al Adler on a dark horse and Cedric Tholes on the cream-colored horse he had ridden to Buchanan's one day.

Fielding wondered why the Argyle foreman would take the trouble to greet him, but he returned the courtesy by saying, "Good afternoon."

Adler, dressed in brown with his white shirt visible, reined his horse so that he could look down on the right side. At the same time, he gave Fielding a view of his free right hand, gloved as always, and his smooth holster and dark-handled gun. "I thought you were in the mountains," he said.

"I was, but I had to come down here on an errand."

Adler frowned and cast a glance at the hitching rail. "Where's your pack string?"

"I had to leave it at the first line camp where I was to deliver goods. Belongs to Dillon. Maybe you know of it."

"I've heard of him, but I don't know all the places yet."

"It doesn't matter much. Your men know where it is."

"I'm sure." Adler looked at the two horses

again. "Have any trouble with the weather?" he asked.

"Not yet, but it can come up at any time."

"I'd say. We just got caught in a hailstorm a couple of miles north, and it gave Cedric a good stinging. Isn't that right, Cedric?"

The man turned his head but did not lower his gooseberry-colored eyes to acknowledge Fielding. "Rah-ther," he said.

Fielding realized it was the only time he had heard Cedric speak.

"Well, we've got to move on," said Adler, "and we don't want to keep you from your work."

"Thanks for stopping."

"Good to see you." Adler touched his hat brim and moved on.

Fielding watched the two men ride away. Good to see him, indeed. For all Fielding knew, Adler had come down this way to see whether Fielding was laid out in a pine box. Whatever the case, Adler would find out soon enough what had happened, if he didn't know already. All Fielding had was the satisfaction of not being the one to tell him — that, and still being on his feet.

He stared at his saddle for a moment, collecting his thoughts. Between the visit with the deputy and the distraction of seeing Adler, his mind had gotten off track. Now it came back. He needed to find another man to work for him.

He left the horses at the livery stable to take on some feed. The stable man said he couldn't think of anyone who needed work, so Fielding went back to the center of town on foot. He asked in the barbershop and the saloon, usually good places for information of that kind, but he had no luck. He went on to the general store, the butcher shop, the blacksmith's, and the train depot. Still without even a recommendation, he trudged back to where he had left the horses.

The stable man said that he had thought of one person who "might could use some work." His name was Baker, and he was no great shakes, but the stable man would send for him if Fielding wanted.

Fielding said he would give it a try. He sat on a bench in the shade outside while a boy ran the errand.

About fifteen minutes later, a tall, slender, pale fellow showed up. He was not wearing a hat, and although he was only about twenty-five, his strawberry blond hair was receding on both sides above his forehead. From the way he moved he seemed to run on low energy, and he talked that way as well.

"Said you're lookin' for help."

Fielding stood up to talk to him. "I am. I need a man to go to the mountains with me and help with my packhorses."

"What's it pay?"

"Dollar and a half a day. We start out today, we call it a full day. Same comin' back."

The man gave a slow nod and seemed to be looking at nothing in particular.

"You know how to work around horses?" asked Fielding.

"Been around 'em." The man raised his head and turned it side to side. "Where are they?"

"The one you'll ride is in here, along with mine. We've got to pick up the rest where I left 'em in the mountains." Thinking that he might as well level with the man from the beginning, Fielding added, "I had to leave 'em there because my other man got hurt. Killed, actually. But it wasn't the horses. Somethin' personal between him and another fella. But they've got nothin' against you."

The man took on his vacant look again. "Lemme have a cirrette and I'll think about it."

Fielding thought he was asking for a cigarette, but the man reached into the

pocket of his loose trousers and took out a
sack of tobacco. He shuffled over to the
bench, sat down, hooked one leg over the
other, leaned forward, and rolled a cigarette.
He lit it and smoked it down halfway, resting his elbow on his elevated knee. Then he
turned, and with his pale eyelids open a
little more than before, he asked, "How
many days we be out?"

"I'd say six, altogether."

He took another drag and said, "I guess I
can do it. I'll go tell my ma." He stood up.

Fielding looked him over again. "If there's
anything you don't have, we'd better get it
before we leave town. You'll need a hat, a
coat, a change of clothes, boots, a bedroll, a
slicker if you've got it."

"I've got all that. I'll be back in a li'l bit."

"I'll wait here. By the way, did I hear this
man correct, that your name's Baker?"

"Yeah. I just don't like to be called Slim."

Baker came back in about half an hour,
wearing a dust-colored hat with a narrow
brim. He was carrying a cotton sack by the
neck, and it didn't look as if it held much
more than a shirt, a pair of trousers, and
maybe a pair of socks.

Fielding eyed the sack. "Is there anything
you need to get?"

"It's all in here," said Baker.

Fielding settled with the stable keeper and brought out the horses. He showed Baker which one he was to ride, and after getting the duffel bag tied on and the man up into the saddle, he adjusted the stirrups by letting them out a couple of inches.

The first night out, the lanky blond man slept under horse blankets with his nose straight up and his mouth open. The second night, after Fielding and his new wrangler had picked up the packhorses and gotten them on the trail again, Fielding gave Baker the bedroll he had made up for the kid. Baker took it without question or comment.

By the second morning, Fielding caught himself getting impatient with the man. Baker seemed to do everything with the least amount of effort possible, as his arms hung at his sides most of the time and his feet did not come very high off the ground. At one point when they were breaking camp, Fielding was rolling up a canvas top pack when Baker appeared at his side and mumbled, "You better come n' see 'bout this horse."

Fielding had heard some thrashing, but the sound had subsided, so he had not quit in the middle of his task. Now he got up and went with Baker to see what the problem was.

The roan horse lay on its side in the midst of foot-high pine and aspen trees. It was wild-eyed and heaving slow, with its chin tucked to its chest as the lead rope held taut between its headstall and a four-inch-thick aspen. Fielding could see at a glance that Baker had given the horse too much slack and it had straddled the rope, tripped itself, and pulled back by nature. After each loud breath, the horse kicked in the air. It rocked to one side, pushed partway up, and fell again.

Fielding shook his head. The knots were pulled tight, and it was hard to get any slack on a horse in this position. Losing no time, he took out his knife and opened it, decided not to risk getting cut or kicked, and cut the rope where it was tied at the tree.

The roan's head jerked back, its legs flailed, and it clambered to its feet in a cloud of dust.

"Why didn't you do something sooner?" asked Fielding.

"I din't wanna get kicked."

Fielding took a short, heavy breath. "Well, go get that horse — no, I'll get him. You untie that rope from the tree. I'll have to splice it later."

Fielding went after the roan and caught him without much trouble. On his way back, he realized he had not told Baker how to tie up a horse. The man didn't show much interest when Fielding did tell him something, and Fielding felt a futility in trying to teach what someone didn't care to learn. Nevertheless, if he was going to get any use out of the man, he was going to have to go through the same things he went through with the kid. He led the roan back to the aspen tree, where Baker was pushing the heel of his hand against the tight knots.

"Here," he said. "Let me show you how to tie a horse so he doesn't get in trouble like this one did. Tie him at this height and give him only a couple of feet of slack." He glanced at Baker, who looked on with indifference. "All right," he went on. "Go ahead and get that piece untied, and we'll get back to work. We'll load this fella later, give him a while to cool down. But he'll be all right." He patted the roan on the neck and moved away.

As they were getting the horses lined out, Fielding made another effort at explaining the work to his new wrangler.

"Notice how none of these horses is very tall. Fifteen hands at the most." He started with this point because he imagined it was something Baker could recognize in his own terms, as the man did not have to lift his foot very high to step into the stirrup. "That's good in a packin' horse, not only so you can get the load on easier but so it doesn't scrape on as many branches. And as you can see, we try to keep the top packs low."

Baker nodded but did not look at the horses.

"Let's get going, then. We'll do the same as yesterday. I'll go first with my four, and —"

"Lemme roll a cirrette first."

Fielding took a quick inward breath. "Go ahead. I'll take a last look around." As he did, he found where Baker had left the tent rope, uncoiled, lying in the thin grass. Words ran through Fielding's mind. *Slow, lazy son of a bitch. Drops everything at his ass.* He picked up the rope and coiled it as he walked back to the pack string. He waited for Baker to finish lighting his cigarette, and then he held up the rope and said, "We need to be more careful, not leave things lying around."

Baker gazed at the rope with an incurious expression.

Fielding stuck the rope into the pannier of Baker's first packhorse and said, "Let's get going, then."

They rode through typical canyon country,

where wildflowers and single blades of grass grew in the sparse soil. They went past a spreading pine tree that grew out of a hillside of gray rocks laid out like a row of fallen columns. At midday they rested in a bottom where a clear, sparkling stream flowed through a grassy little valley, crossing the trail and winding into a rock-wall canyon to the northeast.

After watering the horses there, they started to climb. They passed through a country of high, rocky formations — smooth, yellowish bronze rock that rose in heaps and domes made of huge slabs. Toward late afternoon, the canyon opened into broader country again, with grassland rising away on each side and flanked by hills with dark cedar and pine on the ridges. At a place where a small trickle of a stream came down from the left, Fielding decided to make camp.

Baker held the horses as Fielding untied the pack animals from one another. As Fielding made his way to the horse nearest Baker, he said, "It's good to know your own knots and hitches. You don't always get to undo 'em in daylight and warm weather. By the way, what did you do with that length of rope that got cut this morning?"

"I never could get that sumbitch untied."

"You just left it there?"

Baker shrugged. "What good is it anyway? It was on'y 'bout three feet long."

"By God," said Fielding. "You never know when you need every last piece of rope you've got. I was goin' to splice it onto the length it came off of, but even if I didn't, you use it for something. Untwist it and use the strands, if nothing else."

"It's not goin' anywhere. We can get it on the way back."

The man's careless tone set Fielding off. "Don't make me mad, Baker. I'm just tryin' to get this job done."

For once, Baker's voice rose to something like defiance. "Well, so am I," he said.

Fielding calmed down as he realized that Baker, in his own way, was doing what he thought was a full day's work. "That's all right," said Fielding. "Let's tie these up, and we'll separate the others."

Aggravation came back the next morning when they got ready to mount up. With the loads lighter after the first delivery of supplies, Fielding decided to use the dark horse and the roan for saddle horses for a day. He got the dark horse ready and left it tied as he went to see what was taking the hired hand so long.

Baker stood three feet back from the horse, holding the saddle blankets at waist level.

"What's wrong?" asked Fielding.

"He doan like me."

"He won't give you any trouble. Here, give that to me." Fielding took the pair of folded blankets, gave them a shake, and looked them over for stickers. Then he laid them smooth as a mat on the roan's back. "Now give me your saddle." He swung it up and over, then settled it onto the blankets. Next he reached under the horse, drew up the cinch, and held the ring as he ran the latigo through it. After buckling the back cinch, he held his hand out for the bridle. He tied the halter loose around the horse's neck and drew the bridle up to the horse's nose and mouth. The roan took the bit just fine, and Fielding settled the headstall around its ears. After setting the halter aside, he led the horse out for twenty yards, brought it back, and tightened the cinch until it was snug on three fingers.

"Here," he said, handing the reins to Baker.

The lean man draped the reins around the horse's neck and onto the saddle horn, pulled some of the slack, and then stuck his foot in the stirrup and stepped over.

As soon as he had his seat, the roan went into a rocking-horse buck. The pale-faced rider let go of the reins and grabbed the saddle horn with both hands. After half a dozen bucks, the horse settled down to a stutter step. Baker's right leg came up over the cantle, and he bailed off.

"I'm not gonna ride that sumbitch," he said, pulling off his hat.

"Ah, hell. He's all done buckin'. And he's not that much of a bucker anyway."

"I don't care. I don't wanna sit on him all day long and wonder when he's gonna try it again."

"He didn't even throw you. Just get back on him."

"Not that sumbitch. Not me. Lemme have the one I've been ridin'."

Fielding gave in, figuring he didn't need any more complications. If Baker was afraid, he would communicate it to the horse, and if he chanced to get thrown off, he could get hurt. "All right," said Fielding. "We'll swap him for the brown one."

That evening they pulled into the Harbison camp, which consisted of a shack and a set of corrals. The two line riders were a couple of older punchers whose job consisted in going out and checking on cattle each day. They looked over the horses as the string came in, and Fielding could tell they were inspecting his diamond hitches as well. They helped unpack and hauled their own supplies into the shack.

"Do we get to put the horses in the krell?" asked Baker when both men were in the shack.

"If they tell us to. Same thing with whether we sleep inside or out."

One of the men came out a few minutes later and told them they could put their horses in the last corral. "Looks like you've got oats," he said.

"Oh, yeah, plenty," said Fielding.

"Well, when you've got 'em watered and grained, come on in. Charley's got a pot of beans, and there's not so many mosquitoes inside. Bring your bedrolls in if you want."

Daylight was not yet showing when Fielding woke to the clanking of firewood in the stove. From the man's labored breathing, Fielding could tell it was Charley getting a start on the day.

After breakfast, Fielding walked out into the chilly morning. He had the light, relieved feeling of having delivered the goods he was responsible for and of getting ready for the trip back.

With only their own gear to pack, he and

Baker had the horses ready in about an hour. They waved good-bye to the line riders, and the horses picked up their feet as Fielding started on what he hoped was a quick trip home.

They made good time, but the day warmed up in the afternoon, so Fielding called a rest stop before they went into the narrower, rocky part of the canyon. Following a line of trees up a dry creek bed, he found a water hole that hadn't gone dry. As the horses drank, Baker squatted on one knee and rolled a cigarette.

When the rest was over and Fielding was tying the horses together, he noticed that the canvas bundle of the gear tent had slipped to one side. He pushed it back even and told Baker to tighten it up a little as he tied the other horses. A couple of minutes later, he looked over to see how his wrangler was doing.

Baker stood on his left foot while he had his right against the dark horse's hip. He must have just given a pull, as he sagged for a couple of seconds. Then he straightened up and pulled for all he was worth, his lean frame and thin arms fighting the task. He sagged again and gave it another pull, and the horse broke wind, short and explosive. Fielding almost laughed out loud, and he

188

could imagine someone like Lodge quoting the old saying, "Pull baker, pull devil."

Fielding had told Baker more than once to give the lash rope a steady pull instead of yanks and releases, but he knew by now that his hired hand was no kid and was not likely to change for the better.

"Let me give you a hand," he said. He pulled the rope and tied it off. "That should be good enough."

That evening they pulled into an open spot that looked good for a campsite. Baker tied the horses as he and Fielding stripped them, but he must have been leery of the roan horse and not gotten him snug. Motion caught Fielding's eye, and he turned to see the roan trotting away with the rope trailing on the ground.

"Damn," said Fielding. "You watch these, and I'll go get him." He ran to the bay horse, which he had not yet unsaddled. In a few seconds he untied the neck rope, set his reins, and swung aboard.

He set out on a trot after the roan. He did not want to come galloping up behind the other horse, or it might take off in a game of run and walk. Instead, he kept the bay on a fast trot and gained on the roan. Coming up alongside, he leaned over and got hold of the rope, then dallied it to his saddle horn. The roan did not resist, so Fielding turned both horses and headed back to the campsite on a soft lope.

Just before he got to the trees, he felt a tug on the rope and heard the blast of a rifle. The roan horse went down and jerked the bay sideways, and a second shot crashed.

Fielding jerked the dally loose and threw the rope aside, then kicked the bay into a pounding run until he made it to the trees. He pulled the horse to a quick halt and yanked his rifle from the scabbard. On the first shot he had thought that Baker in a perverse moment had shot at the roan, but he placed the second shot as coming from across the opening, where pine trees grew in a slope of jumbled rocks.

He searched the hillside, which lay in shade, and when he saw movement he placed the object in his sights and fired. It moved again, a man crouched and running uphill. He picked up the target, got a bead on it again, and squeezed the trigger.

The gunshot split the evening, and then the wallop of a bullet hitting a body came echoing back. A man's cry lifted in the air.

Fielding waited. He thought he heard a second voice, the rattle of rocks, a scuffling sound. Dusk began to draw in. Baker had not moved from his position behind the dark horse, which he clutched by the head-stall and packsaddle.

Fielding held still awhile longer. As the evening grew darker, he concluded that the man or men had made it up the hill and gotten away. "I think they're gone," he said to Baker in a low voice. "Whoever it was, I don't think they were shootin' just to get the horse."

Baker's pale face was visible in the dusk. "What are we gonna do?"

"I guess we finish unpacking and keep the horses tied close in. We've got plenty of grain left. We'll use the tent for a tarp to cover the gear, not set up the sleepin' tent."

"What if they come?"

"I don't think they will, but there's no need to give them an easy target. It looks like a night for a cold camp. No fire."

Baker swore under his breath.

"I think they're long gone," said Fielding. "I think I hit one, and the other one's got his hands full trying to get him away. Let's get these animals taken care of and get a bite to eat for ourselves."

In the morning, the dead horse lay where it had fallen. Baker would not even go to the edge of the trees, so Fielding went out and got the halter and rope. When he came back to camp, Baker was smoking a cigarette and had a heavy sulk on his face.

"Look," said Fielding, "I don't like this any better than you do. If they were shooting at anybody, it was me and not you. Like I've already said more than once, I think they're long gone. As for us, there's no point in stayin' holed up here. The sooner we get on the trail and out of this canyon, the better. I think we can make it back to Chug in one long day if we get a move on."

Baker muttered something.

"I didn't catch that," said Fielding.

"I haven't even had a cup of coffee yet."

"Oh, don't worry. We'll have breakfast. If you want to get a fire going, I'll feed the horses." Fielding took a breath and shook his head. "One less to feed anyhow."

They rode into Chugwater at nightfall, coming in by the northern edge of the huge bluffs that overlooked the town. Below them to the east, lights showed in a few windows.

Ten minutes later, they halted the pack string in front of the livery stable and dismounted. Faint light filtered out of the stable door, and out of habit Fielding counted his horses.

"I'm going to put up here for the night,"

he said. "I can take care of the animals, and you can go on home if you'd like. I'll give you this now."

He handed Baker a ten-dollar gold piece, which the man held up close to his face and then dropped into his pocket. He gave the reins and lead rope to Fielding, then took his duffel bag out of the pannier on the white horse.

Out of courtesy more than anything else, Fielding said, "I'll have a little more work comin' up later on. Don't know if you'll be interested."

"I don't think so," said Baker. "I've had enough of wranglin' in the mountains." In his slow way he walked to the bench, sat down, and began to roll a cigarette.

Holding two sets of reins and two lead ropes, Fielding led his eight horses to the stable door.

CHAPTER NINE

The campsite on Antelope Creek looked the same as when Fielding had left it ten days earlier, with the exception that it now lay in midafternoon sunlight and did not have the freshness of morning.

Fielding unloaded all the gear and turned out the horses. The poles were where he had left them, so he set up the gear tent and his sleeping tent. By then he was tired and sweaty, and he could tell he had been on the trail awhile. He went to the creek and had a bath, changed into clean clothes, and washed the ones he had been wearing.

The sun was slipping in the west. He felt worn out and empty but not hungry. After taking a last look at his horses, he went into the small tent and went to bed.

Flies in the tent woke him, and he saw he had slept past sunrise. The sun was beginning to warm the tent, and that was what got the flies going.

He rolled out of bed, pulled on his clean clothes, and went out to check on the horses. Everything seemed to be in order. He moved the picket horses and gave grain to the buckskin in the corral. Having no pressing business in town and being in no hurry to talk to other people, he decided to make some biscuits.

Once he went to the trouble of getting a bed of coals, it was worth his while to make a full batch. A half batch often did not come out as well, and besides, he had plenty of provisions.

First he sliced the amount of bacon he thought he would need to give him enough grease. He laid the slices in the cast-iron skillet and set it on the coals to cook as he got out the dry ingredients and measured them.

In less than ten minutes, the smell of frying bacon seeped out from the covered skillet. Fielding picked up his wooden pothook, a little over two feet long, and lifted the lid. A cloud of steam rose as the crackling sound came alive. Fielding set the lid on a log, took up his fork, and turned the pieces. Then he settled the lid onto the skillet again, to keep the drifting bits of ash from landing in the food.

With the same two-pronged roasting fork, he mixed the dry ingredients he had measured out — flour, baking powder, and salt. He stirred round and round one way, then the other. He shook the metal bowl and leveled the mix, then worked the middle with up-and-down circular strokes.

Setting the dry mix aside, he handled the pothook again and took the lid off the skillet. The bacon had all turned brown and crisp, so he lifted the skillet off the fire and forked all the pieces onto a tin plate. It looked as if he had just enough grease, so he poured it into a tin measuring cup. When the grease rose to the half-cup level, all he had left in the skillet was grains and crumbs of bacon with less than a spoonful of grease, so he set the skillet aside.

Dry heat rose from the coals as he settled the Dutch oven into the place where the skillet had been. With the pothook he set the hot lid on the oven, as the lid fit both cast-iron implements.

Now he poured the grease into the mixing bowl and stirred with the big fork. He stirred and folded, stirred and folded, until he had an even consistency of dough. He set aside the bowl and the fork. With a small piece of cloth he swabbed grease from the skillet and wiped it onto two tin plates. Then with a large tablespoon he dropped gobs of dough — a star of five, with a lump in the center — so that he had six biscuits ready in each plate.

Lifting the lid of the oven, he saw smoke rising from the bottom of the pot, so he set the first plate inside and covered up. He went about tidying up his materials while the first bunch cooked. After ten or twelve minutes, he lifted the lid and turned the biscuits.

By the time he had dug out another plate, served himself a portion of bacon, and poured a cup of coffee, the biscuits had baked a couple of minutes more, so he lifted out the plate and put in the one with the raw dough.

The biscuits tasted smoky with a hint of bacon, plus a bitterness from the tin plate, but they were good, especially parted in the middle with a piece of bacon stuck in. When the first bunch was gone, the second plate was ready to take out. He set it aside to cool next to the bacon, which he covered with a sheet of newspaper. He would eat the second portions cold.

Although he felt better after taking on a meal, the empty feeling still haunted him. He recalled the previous time in this camp, and others before that, when the kid

Bracken had eaten by the same fire. The kid had liked this camp, the horses, the work — Fielding shook his head and tried to get rid of the tightness in his throat. It didn't do any good to dwell on sadness, but he couldn't just forget about the kid.

After two cups of coffee, Fielding cleaned up the camp and put things away. It was time to go back out into the world and see if any news had come this way ahead of him.

He saddled the buckskin and corralled the other horses. After taking a look around the campsite, he mounted up and set out upstream. He crossed the creek sooner than he usually did and took a wide way around, to put a line of hills between himself and Dunvil's camp. Fielding did not know if the wild-bearded man was still around, but if he was, Fielding preferred to wait until later to visit with him.

Angling to the southwest again, Fielding came over the last hill and paused to take a view of the Magpie, Richard Lodge's little spread. Everything looked the same as on his last visit except that the grass was drier, fading to a pale green, and Lodge was not standing in his pasture. The two sorrels were there, standing head to tail and swishing flies.

As Fielding rode down the hill, he saw

Lodge working in the shade of the cabin. It looked as if he was washing something in a tub. Fielding nudged the horse around the front of the house, where he dismounted near the hitching rail.

"Go ahead and tie up," Lodge called out.

Fielding did so, and as he walked around the hindquarters of the buckskin he saw the pile of stones by the cabin door. He could not tell if it had grown any since he had seen it before. Another couple of steps took him into the shade where Lodge was working.

The man had the sleeves rolled up on his drab work shirt, and his dark gray vest was buttoned, the better to keep it from dipping into the water. The tub itself, round and galvanized, rested on the bench that usually sat against the house. Lodge pushed down with a swishing, burbling sound, then amidst the rushing of water he raised up a dripping saddle blanket. Lodge dunked it again, sloshed it up and down, and pulled it out.

Fielding could almost feel it himself, sodden and heavy, and the smell of wet wool carried in the short distance.

"I'll be done in a minute or two," said Lodge.

"No hurry."

Lodge held the blanket up higher, to clear the edge of the tub, and carried it to the top plank of the corral. There he spread it out lengthwise as he had done to the first one. Returning to the bench, he picked up a tin bucket from the ground and dipped it into the tub. He pulled it up and carried it out front, where he poured the water into the earthen bowl around a knee-high cedar tree. It was one of a pair of trees, fifteen yards from the cabin door, that Fielding hadn't paid much attention to because the trees were so small.

Lodge returned for a second bucket of water and poured the contents around the other tree. He took two more trips, then lifted the tub to pour the last of the dirty water into the bucket. This last amount he divided between the two trees.

Fielding thought the man might be done, but he pumped half a bucket of water into the pail, rinsed the tub with it, and poured the water back into the pail. Again he gave an equal portion to each tree. After that he took the pail and the tub around back, where Fielding heard the door open and then close a few seconds later.

Lodge came back, picked up the bench, and set it in its usual place. "Have a seat," he said. "Don't sit in the wet spot." When they were both settled in place, he gave Fielding an expectant look and said, "Well, tell me of your travels."

Fielding took a breath as he thought about how to begin. "Quite a bit happened, as it turned out. Some of it may have gotten back ahead of me."

"Go ahead."

"Well, we got loaded up and pulled out of here the next morning after I saw you last. The first day out, nothin' much to report except we saw Henry Steelyard, who said he was on his way to Rock River."

"I heard he left."

"The next day we got into the mountains, and everything went all right until we started to make camp. And who should show up but that smart-talkin' kid Mahoney and his backup man, Pence."

"Out there?"

"That's right. So Mahoney starts needlin' my wrangler, Ed, and finally goads him into a fight. Ed tries to pull his gun, which he had just bought, and Mahoney puts two bullets through him. I'm sure they were tryin' to get me to play in — Pence even invited me — but I didn't go for it, and I think they didn't want to draw first, just in case everything didn't go right for them. Then they wouldn't be able to say it was self-defense, which they could with Ed. I'll tell you, I felt worthless, knowin' that I was the cause of it and then couldn't do anything about it without gettin' killed myself."

"No need to do that." Lodge moistened his lips as he nodded. "Curious how news travels. All we heard was that Ed died and you had to take him into Chugwater."

"I did that, and while I was at it I hired another man. He wasn't much of a hand, but he did help out, and we got all our goods delivered. Then on the way back, someone ambushed us as we were unloading. A horse got loose and I went after it, and as I was comin' back into camp, someone opened up. Missed me and got the horse."

"Killed it?"

"Dead center. Son of a bitch. Whoever it was, I got a couple of shots at him, and I think I hit him on the second one. I heard him holler. I'm pretty sure someone else was with him and helped him get away. Well, that scared the hell out of my hired hand, but we didn't have any more trouble. We got back into Chug on one long haul the next day."

"Whew," said Lodge as he let out a long breath. "I imagine you've got your suspicions as to who it was."

"I'd guess it was Mahoney and Pence again, but there's no way I can prove anything."

"Purely circumstantial."

"My thought is, they tried it one way, and then they tried it another. But I can't prove without a doubt that it was them, or that they were shootin' at me and not the horse, for whatever difference that would make."

"Interesting circumstances, though," said Lodge, extending his previous comment. "Word is, young hot-blood Mahoney got hurt in some kind of shooting mishap. Didn't kill him but put him out of action. He's laid up at the Argyle, and they had to telegraph for a doctor. Otherwise, I doubt anyone would know that much."

Fielding sorted through what Lodge had just told him. Then he said, "I have to admit, I don't feel guilty about the possibility that I was the one who put a bullet in him. On the other hand, I don't like feeling satisfied about it. Doesn't feel right."

"Take what you can get," said Lodge. "If it was your bullet, then it was his that killed your horse. Not to mention that kid Bracken."

"I know that was a setup, but on the face of it, it was a fair fight. But you're right. I just don't want to feel too satisfied about it.

And besides, even though they'll deny bein' anywhere near, they'll know that I know, and they might want to even the score yet."

Lodge raised his eyebrows. "That's a good practical way of lookin' at it."

Fielding pushed with the heels of both hands on the bench as he looked forward. "I don't like it. I don't like it at all." Turning to Lodge, he said, "What else have you heard?"

"Not much. Maybe one little thing. Joe Buchanan left on a trip to St. Louis. Took his wife and daughter with him, to see about a school for the girl. Finishing school, or something like that. They don't expect him back until just before fall roundup."

"Huh," said Fielding. "When did he leave?"

"Right after I saw you last. About the time you and the kid were settin' out on your trip."

Fielding gave it a thought. "More or less when Steelyard left. Maybe neither of them liked the looks of things."

"Could be. But Buchanan had a reason for his trip, and he didn't leave for good, not like that puncher."

"Half the time, that's what I think I ought to do. Just pack up and leave."

"No one would blame you."

"No, except that I've got work I said I would do. And I wouldn't want to walk out on the rest of you."

"Us?"

"Yeah, you and Selby and Roe."

Lodge had a faraway gaze in his brown eyes and then turned to Fielding. "That's real good of you, and I mean it. But if it comes right down to it, Selby and Roe will look out for themselves. Mark my words. As for me, I can take care of myself, and if I can't, I don't know if you could make a difference, unless you were right there." The older man relaxed his eyes. "Just bein' practical."

"I appreciate it. But I think I'd better stay around at least awhile longer. And by stayin' around, I mean my work, too, which takes me here and there."

"When's your next job?"

Now Fielding gazed into the distance. "In a couple of days I've got a trip to Cogman's Hole, off to the east and a ways north."

"I know the place," said Lodge. "Been over that way once. Is your new swamper goin' with you?"

Fielding laughed. "He said he didn't care for any more wranglin' in the mountains, and I doubt he wants to do any over this way, either."

Lodge tipped his head. "Do you need a hand?"

"Do you mean yourself?"

"Why not?"

"Well, you've got things to take care of, and besides, I wasn't plannin' to take anyone else to begin with. I'm just deliverin' to one outfit, so I won't need but five packhorses, six at the most. It's an easy ride, no mountains or timber."

"You don't want someone along, just in case?"

"Thanks, but I think I'll be all right."

"How about bein' alone in your camp before you leave?"

"Oh, nobody has ever bothered me there."

"You're welcome to put up here," said Lodge.

"Thanks again, but I'm really not worried, especially right around here. And besides, a fellow can't be lookin' over his shoulder all day every day."

"I guess."

Fielding shifted in his seat. "Well, I ought to be movin' along pretty soon."

"Care to stay for noon dinner?"

"Maybe next time."

Lodge perked up. "Say, I just thought of something. Wait here."

He got up from the bench and went

around the back corner of the house as before. Fielding heard the door open and close once, then twice. Lodge came back with something in his hand, and as he held it out, Fielding saw that it was a round, bumpy object with a dry, dull scarlet exterior.

"What's that?" he asked.

"A pomegranate."

"Oh, I've seen them before."

"Take it," said Lodge, with a forward gesture. "I'd guess you've got more visitin' to do, and it might make a nice handsel for someone."

"A what?"

"A gift. A token of goodwill or good luck."

"Oh, I understand." As Fielding took the fruit into his hand, he said, "This must have been shipped in from a long ways off. Where would you come across something like this? That is, if you don't mind my askin'."

Lodge raised his eyebrows and put on a discreet expression. "In a place where meals are served. Fruit of my labor."

Fielding caught the trail west of Roe's place and approached it as if he were coming in from his camp. The road was dusty, and grasshoppers whirred up from the drying grass on either side. On a couple of turns in the road he could see the valley below, greener, and then an intervening hill would close off his view and bring him back to sagebrush, prickly pear, and buffalo grass.

As he rode past the hill that served as shelter on the west side of Roe's yard and buildings, casual sounds drifted on the air — the cackling of a chicken, the bawl of a calf, the thump of a hoof against a plank, the splash of water as someone tossed out the contents of a bucket or dishpan. Fielding looked back to his right and saw the roofed shelter on poles, falling in on one end and leaning toward the same destiny on the other. Into the lane, he rode past the old crippled wagons and the heaps of salvage — posts and planks and wire and tin. The bawling of the calf became louder, followed by a rising chorus of chickens. Now the two gray geese came out, their wings lifted back and their beaks opened in hissing.

Fielding stopped his horse a few yards from the corner of the house. He did not see Roe's wagon anywhere, but he did not know the layout of the place well enough to where it might be parked.

The geese hissed. Not caring to antagonize them, Fielding stayed in the saddle.

"Anyone home?" he called out. The noises in back settled down a notch. He was sure someone was at home, because of the sound he had heard of water being pitched. He called again.

The front door opened with a dull scraping sound, and Isabel stepped out. She was wearing a dark brown dress, and her hair fell loose to her shoulders.

"Oh, it's you," she said. "Just a minute." As she turned and went back into the house, he saw her bare feet.

A couple of minutes later she reappeared, wearing a pair of brown leather shoes that might well have belonged to her mother. "I've been scrubbing," she said. "I hope you don't mind the way I look."

He raised his hat and said, "Fine to me." He waited for her to shoo the geese out of the way, and he dismounted.

As she came to stand facing him, she said, "I was worried about you. We've heard stories."

He wavered, not sure how to begin or how much to tell. With a nod toward the buckskin, he asked, "Shall I tie him up?"

"Oh, yes. By all means. Go ahead."

He tied the reins to the hitching post. Turning to meet her eyes, he said, "The jerky was good."

"I'm glad." She had an anxious, uncertain expression on her face as she hesitated and then said, "I was sorry to hear about that poor boy getting killed. How did it happen?"

Fielding grimaced, but the question was too direct for him to go around. "Two of Cronin's riders met up with us, actually came into our camp, and one of them provoked him into a fight."

Her eyes tightened. "Just like that?"

"I think they were trying to get at me, hoping I'd jump in if they picked on him."

"But you didn't."

He took a quick, deep breath and exhaled. "No, I didn't. It happened all in a moment. I don't know if I could have done anything anyway without getting killed, but I sure felt useless afterward. Poor kid. You know, he wanted to make good."

"I hardly knew him," she said. "Just met him that one time." She blinked, and her dark eyes came back to Fielding's. "And the rest of the trip?"

"I'd like to say it went all right, but it didn't. On my way back, someone shot one of my horses. It seems small in comparison with what happened to the kid, but it's hard to take, too."

She gave a quick intake of breath. "Oh, Tom. Were you alone?"

"I'd just as well have been. I had hired

another man, but he wasn't much good with horses, much less with any real trouble."

"What did you do?"

He raised his eyebrows. "Well, I pulled my saddle gun there, and I threw a couple of shots at where I thought the others came from. I believe I hit a man."

"Then you saw who it was?"

"No, it was too far away, and it was gettin' dark. But I had my hunches, and they match with what I've heard since. I guess one of Cronin's men came back with a bullet wound."

Isabel nodded. "I heard that, too."

"Small coincidence. It was the same fella that got my boy Ed to go for his gun."

She gasped louder than before. "Tom, they wanted to kill you."

"It sure seems that way. Maybe they didn't want to do it bad enough, or they don't have what it takes. I don't know." He was on the brink of saying that he knew they had someone who was capable, but he left it unsaid.

"But why?" she asked.

"I think they want to make an example out of someone. They started with Bill Selby, and now it looks as if they're trying it on me."

"But why you?"

"To begin with, I stuck up for him that day at his place. Then it happened again when we were on roundup, one day we went to get some cattle at the Argyle camp."

"Well, so what if you stick up for someone else?"

"That's what I would think, but it hasn't set well. The way I've heard it, the other side wants to push out all the small-time stockmen and run in another big bunch of cattle for themselves. I think they started with Selby because they thought he would move — sort of a softer touch, you might say. But then I blundered in, and they have to push harder."

She shook her head. "And to do it the way they did. I keep thinking of that poor boy."

"So do I. And a large part of it is my fault. Sure, he got worked up and went for his gun, but if he hadn't been with me, they wouldn't have taken the bother to antagonize him. I got myself into this mess, and he went right along with me, not knowing any better."

"Can't you just get out, then?"

He shrugged. "For one thing, I got into it because I didn't like the unfairness, the idea that someone can run over the top of others because he's got money and connections. That hasn't changed. And even if I did think

I could walk out on Bill Selby and Richard Lodge and your father . . ." He hesitated and went on. "Well, I'd have to pull up everything on short order and go a long ways away. I could cancel the work I've got and say adios. But wherever I ended up, I would know I had been a quitter, and I wouldn't want to live with that."

Her eyes were moist as she held her hands out to him. "I'm glad you're not a quitter," she said, "but no one would blame you if you packed up and left."

He held his hands so that hers lay in his. "That's what Richard Lodge said. But he's the kind of friend I couldn't walk out on." He felt a small tremor and went ahead. "And so are you."

She gave a tender smile. "I have to say, I would be pretty sad if you just walked out, as you put it."

"Maybe I'd take you with me."

She lowered her lashes and looked up at him. "You think so?"

"I don't know. I might have gone too far just then. It's probably too early to talk about that."

She took on an air of simplicity and said nothing.

Fielding thought of something to say. "Speaking of Richard Lodge, he gave me something that he said would make a nice gift."

"A stone? Papa says he collects them, not anything of value but just rocks he picks up in his pasture."

"I've seen him do that. By the way, where is your father? Is he at home?"

"He went to get some merchandise, as he called it. Probably something broken down that he thinks he'll fix up and sell someday."

That was good news, at least his being gone, but Fielding made no comment. He went to his horse and took the pomegranate from the saddlebag, then returned to where Isabel stood waiting.

"Here," he said, holding out the unusual fruit on his upturned palm.

"What is it?"

"A pomegranate."

"Oh, of course. My mother liked them. Is it ripe? Some of them, when they get big and ripen fast, they split open."

"I think this one traveled a long ways."

"Probably so. They wouldn't last if they were split."

"Take it. It's for you."

She took it in her hand and turned it. "Shall we cut it open?"

"Now?"

"Why not? If it's for me, I'd like to share it."

"Well, all right."

"Let's go around back. There's still a little shade."

He followed her to the back step, where she left him for a moment as she went in for a knife and board. When she came out, she pointed at the three-legged stool inside the lean-to.

"Pull that over for a seat if you'd like," she said.

He got the stool beneath him and watched as she undertook the task.

Sitting on the step with the board in her lap, she scored the fruit at the blossom end and split it open. A few scarlet seeds fell on the board, and a wall of them stayed intact on one half of the divide. On the other half, a bumpy yellow layer of pith covered the ruby treasure.

With her thumb she worked off a palmful of seeds, which she poured into his cupped hands. Then she rubbed off a similar amount for herself, and with a shine in her eyes she said, "Here goes." She raised her hand to her mouth.

Fielding popped about a dozen of the seeds in his mouth and mashed down on them, tasting the mixed flavor of astringency and sweetness. "Not bad," he said. "Actually, pretty good."

"Kind of exotic," said Isabel. "Something of a wild taste, like chokecherries, but juicier and not so puckery." She gave a thoughtful look as she ate a few more of the grainy little juice sacs. "Not so much like chokecherry, really. More like currants, though it's been quite a while since I've tasted them. No, I think they taste like pomegranate, and that's it."

"Did you want to save any for your father?"

"Maybe a little, just to taste, but he complains about anything that gets stuck in his teeth. Here, can you get this off?" She handed him the paring knife and pointed at the pale yellow membrane.

As he went about the operation, he asked, "Are you all done with the grain harvest?"

"With my part. The threshing machine moved on north, and some of the crew went with it. I work as long as I can stay with Mrs. Good, but beyond that, it's a little too far from home, and I don't know the people very well."

Fielding nodded. He wondered if the gallant sack jig had gone on with the crew, but he did not ask. If it mattered at all, he would find out without having to be inquisitive.

"That reminds me," she said. "I wanted to give something to you. Would you mind holding this?" She handed him the board with the knife and the open fruit on it.

She went into the house and came out with the brown leather case that Fielding had seen before. As she opened it, the shiny needles came into view.

"I wonder if you'd like one of these," she began.

"Well, um, sure. But I wouldn't want to take something you would need later."

She smiled as she reached to the board in his lap and picked up a few seeds. "You have a lot of things made of canvas, don't you?"

"Oh, yes, I do."

"Do you have a needle like this, or could you use one?" She pointed at the second-largest one, about four inches long, straight with a flare that came back to a spearlike point.

"That's a nice one. I've got one a little shorter, without the flat part. Then I've got a couple of others for regular sewing, of course."

She took it from the case and handed it to him. "A small token from me to you," she said. "Even if you don't use it."

"I might. But I'll keep it here for safekeeping." He took off his hat and poked the needle through his hatband so that less than an inch showed at either end. He put his hat back on his head and said, "Do you like it?"

Her eyes sparkled. "Ever so much. It's like the way the lady assists the knight in the stories."

He set the board next to her on the step and took her hand as he leaned. "You know, you're mighty pretty today. Every day, really, but especially so today."

She laid the leather case aside and stood up as he did. "I'm glad you think so."

As she moved toward him, his hand touched her waist on the side, then moved up to the small of her back. He held her close as their lips met, and although his eyes were shut, he had a clear vision of pomegranate seeds like shiny jewels next to a lance of polished steel.

CHAPTER TEN

When the last packhorse came up onto level ground, Fielding dismounted to check the lash ropes and to give all the animals a rest. The sun had risen to midmorning, and heat rose from the crusty soil at his feet. The valley below looked cool in comparison as the green rangeland stretched away to the west and the north.

With the sun overhead at his back, he did not have to squint to see the country he had passed through — the far hills where he had rolled out before dawn and gathered his horses, the town of Umber where he had loaded the five pack animals in the morning shade of the general store, the trail that led across the broad meadow and up the steep grade to the top.

At the far left of his view, before the rim closed off the valley and foothills, he could imagine Richard Lodge out on the Magpie, maybe saddling one of his two sorrel horses for a ride into town to a place where meals were served. Across in the middle of his view, Isabel would be going through her tasks. And back in town, the white speckled horse and the brown one were corralled at the livery stable for a few easy days.

The five he had with him were all doing fine, and the packs rode even and snug as he pulled at the lashes. The buckskin, which walked at his side, gave a stamp of the foot. Fielding turned and passed the reins to his left hand. It was the third or fourth time the saddle horse had stamped. Up and around came the tail, swishing both ways. Fielding moved to the off side, transferring the reins again. There he saw a horsefly rising and settling, rising and settling, just behind the saddle blanket and on the fore part of the hip. The large black-and-gray insect was easy to pick out against the tawny hide.

Fielding ducked under the horse's neck, wormed his hand into the saddlebag for his gloves, and pulled them out. He slipped the left one onto his hand as the buckskin stamped again and swished its tail. Fielding came up on the other side of the animal and found the horsefly circling above and coming down in the same place. As he tightened his grip on the reins, the horse braced itself. Down came the gloved hand,

and the large fly, the size of the last joint of a man's little finger, fell motionless to the dirt.

After taking a last look at the valley and casting another glance over his pack string, Fielding led the buckskin to the front of the line. He took the lead rope from where he had draped it over the neck of the gray horse, and after positioning the buckskin he mounted up. With a click-click sound, he got the pack train into motion.

Travel across the flats was hot and dry. The wind up here on top had a parching quality, and it raised bits of dust and chaff from the wheat stubble as Fielding rode past the fenced parcels. Most of this country was open range, where the short grass was turning thin and curly, and the longer grass had dry flags and seed heads.

From time to time he saw cattle, many of them with the familiar brand of interlocking diamonds. Not all of the Argyle cattle were on summer range, that was for certain, and in another month or so, this range would be sere and brittle. Come winter, most if not all of the growing Argyle herd would be grazing in the valley.

Fielding continued riding east-northeast. He figured he had about twelve miles to cross, plus a ways after that until he came to water, so he kept his eyes out for a place to water the horses in the meanwhile.

Most of the wheat farms lay behind him now, and the country was wide open. An occasional hawk soared on the air currents above, while here below, grasshoppers took to their wings and clacked like a wind-up toy. Fielding startled little gray birds out of their shade in the sagebrush, and at one point he came within two hundred yards of three buck antelope. As he saw their curved horns and black cheek patches, he recalled that it was the time of year when the bucks ran together and the does were with their fawns.

Two light green trees in the distance suggested water, so he veered northeast toward them. After a mile, they still looked a mile away. He rode on.

As he came within a quarter of a mile of the actual site, he saw that the trees grew on the bank of a man-made reservoir. Closer, he could see the depression itself, where most of the water that had gathered in the spring was gone. Cakes of dried mud led down to a water hole ten feet across and two inches deep, with a skim of bugs and green matter. Fielding watered the crowding horses one by one, then led them back up onto the flat and off in the direction he wanted to go.

He had to travel southeast along the rim to find the descent he was looking for. It was a narrow trail threading down through grayish tan bluffs, formations of layered sandstone with pine and cedar growing on ledges, in clefts, and on the slopes. He rode down in, past a turret-shaped rock on his left, which gave the effect of a gateway as the trail wound past it and led into Cogman's Hole.

The Hole, as it was called, was a broad, grassy basin enclosed on all sides but the east by a rim of bluffs such as the one he was going down through. The country below him was light green, then took in a darker hue that shaded into blue as the grassland stretched away beneath a thin cover of afternoon clouds.

Fielding twisted in the saddle to see how his animals were doing. They shifted and turned as each one found its footing, the off-white packs moving like train cars on a bad stretch of road bed. Shod hooves made pocking, grinding sounds on the rock and large-grained sand. Sweat trickled down Fielding's back, and a dryness came to his mouth, but he was glad to be making his way down into the Hole.

At the bottom, he followed the base of the

slope that came from the foot of the bluffs on his left. The shadow of the rim was beginning to stretch out, but it would be a while until Fielding and the horses would have the benefit.

He rode on to a place he had in mind, where a small creek came down from the rim and threaded a row of trees across the grassland. Near the base of the slope he found the spot, a well-worn area where roundup outfits had camped. The ground was bare and hard-packed, and a person had to look out for the stubs of old picket stakes, but it was a good site. It had two campfire circles, plus a pool where men had built a low dam of rocks to back up the water.

Fielding stripped the horses and watered them, brushing their wet, shiny backs with a burlap bag. He picketed two horses and belled the rest, then set the packs in a row with saddles on top and the pads draped over, wet side up to dry. Later he would cover the provisions and gear with the tent as a tarpaulin.

He had to walk along the slope quite a ways to gather firewood, but it was a peaceful job. He meandered in the lengthening shadows, keeping an eye out for snakes as well as deadfall, and casting an occasional glance at the horses.

The smoke from the campfire came in thick, pungent puffs until the blaze took hold. When the sticks burned down to coals, Fielding set the skillet on a triangular layout of rocks. As he often did, he had brought fresh meat for the first night out, so he enjoyed the sound and smell of searing steak as he sat on his bedroll and waved away wisps of smoke. Camping by water in this part of the year meant mosquitoes, and it was worth enduring a little smoke to keep the whiners away.

Before going to bed, Fielding went out to check on his picket horses. They were both doing all right, and he could hear the four different bells of the horses that were grazing farther out. The moon was up, growing to a half-moon, and the night was clear. Fielding had a sense of where he was. Cogman's Hole ran about twenty miles west to east and fifteen miles south to north. He was on the western edge, roughly halfway along the rim that curved around.

As he walked back toward camp, the shadow of a large bird passed over and beyond him, and as his heart jumped he heard the soft flap of wings. The surge of alarm came from deep within, and his head felt vulnerable. Then his rational half came back into control. He had his hat on. It was just a bird of the night, must have been an owl, looking for small furry creatures beneath the prairie moon.

Back in camp, he set up the tepee tent with its jointed pole. He could hear the bells on the horses as he rolled out his bed, and he did not worry about much of anything as he closed his eyes.

Morning broke fresh and clear as Fielding sat on his bedroll and drank his coffee. He figured he had about ten miles to go until he came to Wald's sheep camp. If he got there early enough, he could turn around and come part of the way back the same day.

He gathered the horses, rigged them, and put on the packs. He was sweating by the time he mounted up, but a light breeze cooled his shirt and his cocked hat as he set out on the day's ride. Relaxed, he heard the song of a meadowlark rise above the prairie as the horse hooves clomped and swished through the grass.

Fielding and his string rode into the sheep camp in early afternoon. Wald himself lived up by Fort Laramie, so he had a couple of hired hands at this place — a camp tender as well as a herder — and the tender was usually at camp alone. As Fielding rode into the dusty site, a long-haired black-and-white dog came out of the shade and barked until the tender emerged from the tent and rasped a couple of words.

Fielding recognized the tender as Prew, a beardless person with a bulldog face and a trunk that went down like a barrel from the shoulders to the hips. Fielding had heard of women who worked and lived their whole lives as men, among men, without anyone knowing the difference, and he wondered if Prew was one of these. The camp tender was not unfriendly, just offish in an intangible way, so Fielding preferred to unload the supplies and be gone.

"Whatcha got?" asked Prew, in the same harsh voice.

"Salt in the first one, grain in the second, provisions in the other three, my stuff on top."

Prew said, "Get out of the way" to the dog, then came around to stand by as Fielding untied the knots.

In a few minutes, Fielding was emptying the panniers. The camp tender handled fifty-pound sacks of salt and sixty-pound sacks of grain with no trouble, and the process moved right along. When Fielding had all the camp goods unloaded, he distributed his own gear and got things tightened down again.

He looked at the sun, which had moved over but was not slipping yet. "Plenty of time left," he said. "If I can water these horses, I can get started back."

"Good enough," said Prew. "Glad you made it. Sheep was runnin' low on salt."

As Fielding put the sheep camp behind him, he was glad to be on his way. He didn't mind sheep, though sometimes the tallowy smell hung in his nostrils, and he didn't mind sheepherders. They worked for their living, and they took good care of their horses, fed them well and hardly ever pushed them to more than a fast walk. All the same, he was relieved to have this job done and to be traveling light.

He made good time and was able to camp in the same spot as the night before. He didn't get the horses picketed until sundown, and when he did, he paused to appreciate the yellow-and-orange sky above the rim as the shadows laid a velvet softness on the rocks and grass and trees along the slope.

He fed the last of his own grain to the horses in the morning, and he had them all watered and loaded before the day had warmed up. With the sun at his back, he led the pack string out of camp. Before long the trail curved so that the sunlight fell on his left side, and without the benefit of a breeze, he continued sweating. He hoped for a breeze up on top.

Without dismounting he rested the horses for a couple of minutes before starting up the grade. The trail was not very steep to begin with, but after the first quarter-mile stretch it made a turn and began to climb at a sharper pitch. The horses behind him snorted and blew, and their hooves crunched in the hard, grainy path as the party moved uphill in order.

Fielding gazed at the sandstone wall he was traveling through. Tiny ledges supported tufts of grass and small bushes. Cedar trees grew in narrow clefts. Up where the trail turned again, the rock that had seemed like a gateway loomed on the right. If a man watched the land close up for too long, things seemed to move on their own, so he let his eyes rove around. He looked across empty space at other sections of the wall. He shifted in the saddle and watched the horses and their packs laboring up the slope behind him. His eyes came back to the trail ahead, and still a rock seemed to move.

He stopped the buckskin, a habit of second nature when he saw something out of place. He had a full awareness that this was a poor place to stop the horses, where they would have to stand leaning forward and work to keep from slipping on the loose surface. But rocks did not move.

He slid from the saddle, wrapped the lead rope around the saddle horn, and lowered the reins to the ground. The trail was barely wide enough for him to walk sideways past the horses, but he needed to get to the second set of panniers. The movement he had seen was up the trail on his right, beyond the turret-shaped rock. If someone had ducked out of sight, the person would have a hard time seeing what the delay was. He would have to wait.

Fielding reached into the pannier and pulled out a burlap sack. After making sure that it was open at both ends, he edged back to the first packhorse, the gray one. Crouching, he lifted the front left foot of the horse and slipped it through the open sack. Bunching the burlap so that it resembled a sash or large band, he twisted it once, twice, three times, then fitted the other hoof through the opening at the other end.

With the horse hobbled, he backed out and stood up. He let out a long breath and hoped everything held. The buckskin was good at staying ground-hitched, and between the lead rope and the hobbles, Fielding hoped to have this train pretty well stalled where it was.

He unstrapped his spurs and put them in the pannier where he had taken out the burlap sack. Feeling around, he laid hold of a length of quarter-inch rope. With it in his hand, he made his way to the end of the line and tied the sorrel to the back end of the dark horse. Then he went around the sorrel and crossed the trail. After drawing his six-gun, he moved to the base of the rock tower and peered over. A small canyon fell away, steep but not impossible. If he could get around the formation without dislodging too much loose rock, he might be able to come up on someone. Meanwhile, he hoped nothing would spook the horses.

Once over the edge, he saw a game trail about fifteen yards below. It looked like his best bet. He picked his way down to the trail and, leaning in toward the declivity of the canyon, took slow, quiet steps forward. He knew that sounds carried upward in places like this, so he kept an eye out for rocks that would slip beneath his feet.

Things always looked different from below. He could not see the trail above, only the rocks that overlooked it. He had no idea which crevice, if any, might hold a man in waiting.

The heat of the sun was stronger here, where it reflected off the rocks and crumbling soil. The smell of sage and dust came to his nostrils. A fly landed on the back of his sweating hand, and he made a small motion to shake it away. A velvet orange ant climbed across an open space of dirt an arm's length away. Tufts of goat-beard grass held on to small knobs of earth, and daggerlike clumps of yucca rose at eye level. The rocks passed above him.

Though it seemed like an hour, he knew it had been but five minutes since he had slipped away from the trail. He squinted in the heat. Then as he looked up he stopped in midstep and set his foot straight down. Above in the rocks he saw a pair of scuffed brown boots sticking out of the legs of a pair of brown canvas trousers. A man was still waiting.

Fielding passed below, taking more care than ever to keep from making noise. In another minute he could no longer see back around a buttress of rock that jutted out, but he marked the spot in his mind. Now he looked for a way to climb out. He holstered his gun and forged ahead.

Another three or four minutes took him up out of the canyon on his left and onto the ledge, where a faint breeze cooled the sweat on his face. He was still not up on the flat itself, but the trail was not so steep here. He sidestepped down to the trail itself. Staying close to the edge where the grass grew and where the rocks would keep him from being seen, he worked his way back. After about sixty yards, he climbed up onto a sandstone ledge. From there he walked forward in a crouch, with his hat tipped to keep the sun out of his eyes.

When he came to a crevice, the man was not there. If he had not sneaked away, he was in the next one. Fielding eased down into the opening, came up on the other side, and crossed the next rocky surface with his gun drawn. As the crevice came into view, the scuff of Fielding's boot heel caused the man to jerk around and sit up in a kneeling position.

Fielding would have recognized him sooner if had been wearing his black hat, but he was wearing an older gray one with a smaller crown and brim. Between that and his black vest and dust-colored work shirt, the man looked like a giant horsefly. As Fielding focused on the shaded face, he saw that the usually dull-lidded eyes were open in surprise, and the fellow's mouth hung open. Now Fielding had an answer to the question of whether Foote had gone north with the harvest crew.

"What are you lookin' for?" asked Fielding.

"Nothin' much."

"That's not what it seems like."

Foote regained some of his arrogance right away. "You don't own this place," he said.

"Neither do you." Fielding waved his six-gun. "I don't like someone lyin' in wait for me on the trail."

"How do you know what I was doing?"

"Don't act stupid on me. Get up out of there, and keep your hand away from your gun."

"Who do you think you are, giving me orders?"

"You know damn well who I am, or you wouldn't be hiding here. Now get up."

The sluggard rose to his feet.

"Now climb down onto the trail here."

"What for?"

"For a while. Now move."

The other man looked at the gun and did as he was told. With pistol in hand, Fielding scooted and jumped down to face him.

The big man tipped his head back and to

234

one side. "What are you goin' to do now?"

Fielding holstered his gun. "I'm going to tell you something. I don't know what you're up to, but I don't like someone spying on me. Last trip I went on, I had a man get killed."

"Then you ought to be careful."

"If I wasn't, I wouldn't have gotten the drop on you. This time's a warning. I hope there isn't a next time, but if there is —"

Foote raised his head again and looked past Fielding. The sound of horse hooves caused Fielding to turn around, and again he saw something that didn't match at first. Coming down the trail on one horse and leading another was George Pence, his high-crowned hat and blocky form in full sun.

Fielding kept his eye on the rider. As long as the man kept his hand on the reins of the horse he was leading, he wasn't likely to draw his gun.

No one spoke until the horses came forward and stopped, at which time Pence called out in a loud voice, "Well, if it ain't the packer, out here on foot. What's gotcha down?"

Fielding watched the man's hand as he answered, "Does this lunk ride with your outfit now?"

"Might be. Why should you care?"

"I caught him hiding here, waitin' for me to come up the trail."

Pence gave a hollow laugh. "Oh, go on. His horse got away from him, and I told him to wait here in the shade while I went and got it."

"Did you tell him that people get shot when things go wrong?"

Pence's face tightened. "What do you mean by that?"

Fielding had a good hunch that Pence thought he was referring to Mahoney, but he decided to leave that part unsaid. "I told him one of my men got killed on the trail. I didn't tell him you were there, but now that it looks like he rides with you, maybe he should know. The next time, it might be the other way around."

"This man's new at this work," said Pence. "That's how his horse got away. But if someone pulls a gun on him, he's got a right to shoot back."

"Anyone does." Fielding tossed a casual glance at the man in question. "He'd do better to keep his gun in his holster, though, and work on the cow-punchin' part."

Now Foote spoke. "I'll take you on any time, mister horseman, and fists is my favorite way."

"Hope for the best," said Fielding. "If I

was to wish something for you, it would be that you found another outfit to ride for. Unless you like to look for trouble, which maybe you do."

"I don't need your advice."

"But you'd do well to take it. This outfit shoots and gets shot at, and I don't know how much of that you've got in you." The other man did not answer, so Fielding turned to Pence. "Be careful about what you say or do around this one," he said. "Sooner or later, he might turn stool pigeon on you."

Pence tipped his head, with a slow motion of his chin. "Worry about your own problems, and I'll worry about mine."

Fielding went back to his horses. Seeing nothing out of order, he put on his spurs, took the hobbles off the first packhorse, and got the string moving uphill again. He did not see the other two men on his way to the top, and once he was out on the flats, he saw only grass and sagebrush for miles around.

The valley lay before him as he paused before taking the pack string down. Everything looked in place, from Lodge to Roe to Selby, down to the railroad line and the town, and off to the north across undulating grassland to the Argyle headquarters, where punchers came and went. Fielding turned in the saddle, saw the horses and packs in order, and touched a heel to the buckskin. The horse shifted and sidestepped his way down the gash in the rim, coming out at the bottom where the chokecherries on the left were turning red.

As usual, the horses seemed to know they were on the last stretch. The buckskin picked up his feet, and the rest fell in at the same fast walk. Fielding pulled down the brim of his hat to shade out the mid-afternoon sun. One stop at the livery stable, and he would be on his way to camp.

As he turned into the main street of town, Fielding saw two horses tied in front of the post office. They looked like the horses he had seen Adler and Cedric riding when they came down the street in Chugwater. The dark horse carried a scabbard with a rifle. Fielding took a closer look in the shade of the overhang, and there sat Cedric on the bench, opening a letter with what looked like a paper knife. His yellowish white hair was conspicuous in the subdued light. At that moment, Adler walked out of the post office empty-handed and made a small wave of greeting. Fielding waved in return.

The two men were still there when Fielding came back from the livery with the two fresh horses tied to the end of the string. Adler in his white shirt and brown hat and vest stood close to the street and seemed to be taking stock of Fielding's horses. Cedric was perusing the letter.

Fielding thought it might be an opportune moment to call Adler's hand in front of Cedric. He reined the horse toward the sidewalk and dismounted before he had a chance to talk himself out of it.

Adler's voice came from the edge of the shaded sidewalk. "Afternoon, Fielding."

"Good afternoon. If you've got a moment, there's something I'd like to mention."

"Go ahead." Adler took out his silver watch and began to wind it. When he looked up, Fielding spoke.

"Well, not to beat around the bush, I need to say that I don't care for your men harassing me."

Adler paused in his winding and fixed a stare on Fielding. "I understand that the kid went for his gun first. You even told the deputy that, if I'm not mistaken."

"He did, but it wouldn't have happened at all if Mahoney and Pence hadn't shown up at my camp to begin with."

Adler waved his eyebrows. "They were on open range as much as you were."

"A man's camp is his camp. But that's not the only incident anyway."

"What other was there?" The man's voice had a dead-level tone to it.

Fielding thought Adler was waiting to counter him about the shoot-out when the roan horse got killed, but he skipped to the more recent flare-up. "In addition to the time I got jumped and couldn't see for sure who it was, I had another run-in. Someone was lurkin' in the rocks when I was comin' back from Cogman's Hole earlier in the day, and when I surprised him, your man Pence came along to get him off the hook."

"What do you mean, lurking?" Adler put the watch away and pulled his right glove onto his hand.

"He was lyin' in wait for me, right off the side of that narrow trail. So one time I'm off in the west, and the other time I'm over east, and wherever I go, I run into your men watchin' my trail."

Adler gave a slight turn so that his gun and holster came into view. His voice was steady as he spoke. "They say you're a good hand, Fielding, and you do your work. Even if you're thick with people like the junk collector. But watch what you say. If my men are out on the range in one place or another, they're lookin' after Argyle cattle."

Cedric was folding up his letter.

Adler went on. "Tell me, then. Who was it you caught lurking, as you put it?"

"A new hand of yours, name of Ray Foote."

Adler laughed. "A hand named Foote. A galoot who's still learning not to fall off a horse. Do you think you have anything to fear from him?"

"To tell you the truth, sir — no, I don't. But he gets his orders from somewhere."

"He didn't get that one from me." Adler paused. "Anything else?"

"Not at the moment." Fielding led the buckskin away, mounted up, and lined out his string. As he looked back, he caught a glance of the two men on the sidewalk. Cedric seemed to be watching the white horse on the end, while Adler seemed to be taking them all in, one by one.

CHAPTER ELEVEN

Fielding sat on a heap of folded canvas with his back resting against one of the two fireside logs. In his lap he had a short length of rope on his right thigh and the end of a longer piece on his left. He untwisted the strands for about six inches back from each end, then stubbed the two pieces together with the strands splayed out and alternated as they met and crossed one another. With a piece of string he tied the strands of the right piece to the tight twisted part of the left piece. Then he rotated the rope on his right so that the strands separated in tense curls, and he tucked the first strand from the left piece over and under a strand on the right. He repeated the operation with the other two strands, then did all three strands again. With the right side finished, he turned the whole rope around and spliced the other side, now on his right. When he was done, he had what he had learned to call a short splice. How strong it was would be seen when a horse pulled against it.

Hoofbeats called his attention to the path that came into his camp from the main trail. Fielding set aside the rope and stood up. As the rider came past the last box elder tree, Fielding recognized the build and posture of Bill Selby. The man slowed his horse from a lope to a walk but did not stop until he was within a few yards of the campfire area. Dust rose to stirrup level, and the horse was barely stopped when Selby swung down and stood away with the reins in his gloved hands.

His face was flushed, and his lower eyelids were puffy as usual. His light blue eyes were full of worry, and his jaw hinges bulged as he took in a deep, nervous breath through his nose.

"We've got trouble, Tom. Big trouble." His chest rose as he breathed again. "Richard Lodge has been shot."

"The hell. Was he hurt bad?"

"Hurt? He was killed."

The words stunned Fielding, and he took a few seconds to absorb their impact. "Killed? When did this happen? Where?"

"I went out to his place yesterday afternoon. It looked as if it had happened earlier in the day. He was lyin' facedown in the dirt, right in front of his cabin. Both horses in the corral. Hoofprints in front, looked like one rider, but no sign of anyone gettin' off a horse. The deputy's been out there, but he says he doesn't have much to go on."

"Yesterday, you say."

"That's right. I didn't know you were back, or I would have looked you up. But I was busy with all of this until late last night anyway."

"Yesterday," Fielding repeated. "I was coming back from Cogman's Hole. Along about ten to eleven in the morning, probably closer to ten, I ran into that jackass Ray Foote. Turns out he works for Cronin now, and George Pence was along with him. Came out of the greasewood a few minutes later."

"That's probably about the time someone shot Richard." Selby's eyes were ablaze with worry. "I tell you, Tom, this is bad. Real bad for all of us. Everyone liked Richard except you-know-who." Selby looked around as he finished his sentence.

Fielding gave a slow shake of the head as he felt his spirits sinking. Lodge was dead, never to pick up another stone in his pasture, and just as he had said, Selby was worried about himself. It took Fielding a long moment to break through the numbness and find words.

"It's bad, all right. Bad for everyone, but especially Richard. He lost the last thing a man can lose." Fielding looked off into the distance and came back. "I saw Adler in town when I came through yesterday afternoon. Put it at three or so. He was in front of the post office with his tagalong Cedric, who'll probably give him an alibi for the whole day. But it would have been plumb easy for Adler to go out there by himself, shoot Richard down in cold blood, and either go back to the Argyle or meet up with Cedric in town. It'll be hard to prove, but I'd bet ten to one it was Adler."

Selby winced, and his eyes moved to the side. Fielding had the impression that Selby did not like to name names or even hear them spoken. As for Fielding, he could picture Adler as he had seen the man the day before, standing straight up in his white shirt and brown vest, with his gun and holster in plain view.

Selby spoke. "Everyone's got to step careful here. The deputy asked me if anyone had anything against Richard, and I told him about the set-to over in their camp that day. I think we need to let him ask the questions."

"And what do you plan to do?"

Selby blinked a couple of times. "We need to hang together, Tom, and be careful. No one sticks his neck out until we know what the deputy finds out."

"You can pretty well predict that, can't you?"

"I don't know. If he asks around, maybe someone saw something."

"Sure. Like the fellow up in Johnson County." Fielding did not think he had to tell the rest, as it was well known how a man had seen Frank Canton and heard shots at ten in the morning at the place where Johnnie Tisdale was shot in the back and his two wagon horses and little dog were shot as well. The witness was so scared that he jumbled his testimony at the inquest, and Canton walked free. And that was a case in which there was a known witness. In others, like the case on the Sweetwater, the witnesses disappeared.

Selby did not answer, so Fielding spoke again. "Are his two horses still standing in the corral?"

"Oh, no," Selby answered. "I took them to my place so they'd be taken care of." He said it with the tone of someone who had performed his expected duty.

"Saddle, too?"

"Well, yeah. He had two of 'em. No sense in leavin' 'em where someone could get his hands on 'em."

Fielding decided not to pursue that line any more at the moment. "So they've got him in town?"

"That's right." Selby nodded his head in his officious way. "Funeral at ten in the morning, tomorrow. I was afraid you might miss it."

The group that gathered at the cemetery consisted of Selby, Roe, Isabel, Leonora, Fielding, and Mullins. The wheat farmer would probably not have shown up except that he had been asked to work in the café for a couple of days while Leonora took some time off.

After the service, which was short and not very comforting, the group left the coffin next to the open hole and the pile of dirt and went to the parlor of the house where Leonora rented a room. Selby had arranged for cake and cold meats to be brought in from the café, and Mullins tended to the sideboard where the food was laid out.

A desolate feeling pervaded the room, and no one spoke much. When everyone had eaten and set their plates aside, Mullins poured coffee in china cups. The group sat on upholstered chairs arranged in an oval, and as there were three unoccupied, Mullins poured himself a cup of coffee and sat in respectful silence.

"He was a good man," said Selby.

Fielding started to speak, then cleared his throat and said, "The best."

Roe sniffed, rubbed his nose both ways, and said, "He was. Never a cross word to his friends, never owed a man a nickel."

"Didn't complain," Selby added.

Leonora, still wearing the black veil she had worn to the cemetery, took a slow breath and sat up straight. She had a tremor in her voice as she said, "He was all that, and more. Generous, kind, intelligent." She set her cup on its saucer, and it rattled until she stilled it. With her chin raised, she said, "He didn't deserve to die that way."

Selby and Roe looked at their own coffee cups, but Isabel's eyes rose and met Fielding's.

"I remember the last time I saw him," she said. "He played a few songs for us."

"Oh, he was fond of music," Selby put in. "Wrote a few airs himself."

"He liked birds," said Fielding, caught up in the sadness of the moment. "Songbirds." Then he felt silly for having said what he did.

"It's too bad," Mullins offered. "A man in his prime . . ." Mullins's sentence trailed off.

Fielding steadied his voice as he spoke again. "He offered to ride along with me to Cogman's Hole. I should have let him go. We would have still been up on the flats at that time."

Leonora set her cup on the saucer and held the two pieces with both hands. "It wouldn't have mattered," she said in a bitter tone. "The cowards would have gotten him one way or another."

Selby and Roe did not look up, and an uncomfortable silence hung in the room until Fielding said, "I think you're right. The part I left out was that he offered to go along for my sake. He wasn't worried about himself."

"That was Richard," said Leonora. "More of a man than the ones that came looking for him."

Selby drew himself up as if he was about to speak, and Fielding was afraid he was going to say that it looked as if only one man did the job, but then Selby relaxed and said nothing. Leonora did not speak again, either. A few minutes later, Selby stood up and took leave. Roe followed, taking Isabel with him. Leonora withdrew, and Fielding helped Mullins carry the leftover cold food to the café.

Fielding woke to the sound of birds fluttering and squawking. As he peeked out of the flap of his pyramid tent, he could see the young cottonwoods against the gray sky of morning. A flock of starlings had moved in, and the birds were traveling back and forth across the creek, between the cottonwoods and the box elders. There wasn't much food for them here, he thought. Even if he had a shotgun, it would not be easy to run off a flock like this one. He would just endure them and not leave out anything for them to drop their deposits on. Before long they would move on, and if they followed the creek they would find a patch of chokecherry bushes, where they would strip all the fruit before it ripened. After that they could go ten or fifteen miles north and plunder a wheat field.

He tended to his horses and got a fire going, then boiled some coffee to go with his cold biscuits. Nothing tasted good, and he had an irritated, dissatisfied feeling mixed in with the dread and sadness. If there was nothing good about Bracken's death, there was even less so about Lodge's, and brooding in camp alone had not improved his state of mind.

After breakfast, he put his few things away and saddled the bay horse. With his other horses corralled, he left his camp to the starlings and rode off across country. His plan was to visit Selby first and then Roe, and he didn't want to ride past the junk collector's on the way.

When he rode into Selby's yard, the man came out to meet him. Selby looked ready for the day with his hat on and his gloves in his hip pocket, but he seemed fidgety as he said good morning and gave a smile.

Fielding returned the greeting and dismounted.

Selby sounded as if he was making an effort to appear cheerful. "What's on your mind today, Tom?"

"More of the same, I'd guess. And yourself?"

"Likewise. Are you goin' out on another trip before long?"

"In a couple of days."

"Well, that's good. Keep you busy, get you away so your mind isn't on all this other stuff."

"It seems to follow me."

"Oh." Selby drew his mouth together as he closed off the sound.

Fielding tried to gauge the man but

couldn't. It seemed as if Selby had reconsidered things and was now avoiding both comment and confrontation. Fielding spoke. "I'll tell you, Bill, I dropped in to see if we could come up with some idea of how we were going to do things."

"Uh-huh." Selby's eyes had a blank expression.

Fielding went on. "You've got an idea what I mean."

Selby blinked. "Well, no. Actually, I don't. You'll have to fill me in."

"What I mean is, you've been sayin' all along that we need to stick together, which is even plainer now than before."

"It's true I've said that —"

Fielding narrowed his gaze on the man. "Do you think you're having second thoughts about it?"

"Well, no, not exactly."

"I'm wonderin', then, if anyone's got an idea, or a plan, on what we're going to do as a group. I don't have any ideas myself, but I don't have holdings like the rest of you, so I may not see things the same."

Selby shrugged. "Maybe."

Fielding went on. "I can't help thinking that we should have done something rather than just wait. Even Richard —"

"It's too late for him," said Selby. "He

wasn't worried about himself, but maybe he should have been."

"Seems to me we all should be."

"You'd be a fool not to. If a man doesn't look out for himself, who's going to?"

Fielding could almost hear Lodge's voice. *Mark my words.* Maintaining his calm, he said, "Then I guess each of us has to have his own plan first."

Selby put up a matter-of-fact expression as he said, "I think you've got to start there."

"I see." What Fielding actually saw, he didn't state. Cronin's men had started by making an example out of Selby, had raised the stakes when they moved on to Fielding, and had raised them even higher when they took care of Lodge. Now Selby did not want them to come back to him, and he wanted to avoid an alliance with Fielding that might bring on more retribution. Fielding looked down and then up again. "Do you have a plan for yourself?" he asked.

"Not yet. But I might be workin' on one."

"Well, I won't ask about it."

"Oh, it's not a secret," said Selby right away. "Just not very definite." After a short pause, he added, "I'm thinkin' I might pull up my stakes here."

"Sell out?"

Selby tipped his head. "I might sell what I

can, take what I can. But like I said, none of that's definite yet."

Empty homesteads. Just what Cronin wanted. "By the way," said Fielding, "do you have an idea of what's going to become of Lodge's place?"

"The Magpie? I heard yesterday evenin' that a crazy man was camped out there."

"Dunvil, the anarchist?"

"I believe that's him. I haven't met him myself, but Richard mentioned him. Sounds crazy as a loon."

"He might be." Fielding was about to ask Selby where he heard it, but he held his question. He did not think he had that level of confidence with Selby anymore.

The knowledge that Dunvil was camped out at the Magpie caused Fielding to reconsider the sequence of his visits. By the time he had ridden half a mile from Selby's place, he had decided to go visit the wild man and find out if he knew anything. Turning his horse to the south, he set off across country.

He came onto the homestead acreage a little to the east of where he usually did. From his position he could see three of the four conical rock piles that marked the corners of the property, while the house and stable and corral lay uphill on his right. At first he saw no signs of occupation, and then he noticed the mule picketed on the grass out beyond the stable. With a light movement of the reins he put the bay horse in the direction of the house and yard.

As he rode up the hillside and came into the yard, he had a feeling of emptiness from knowing that Lodge would never tend to his place again. The two little cedar trees stood in an area of sparse grass and hard earth, and the heap of stones by the front step looked purposeless. The door of the house was closed, as were the corral gate and the stable door. Fielding wondered how long it would be until weeds began to take over.

He called out, "Anybody here?"

He waited amidst the silence of inert stones and weathered lumber. Not a breeze stirred. He called again.

The squeak of hinges and the scrape of wood sounded from the stable. The door moved outward, and Dunvil stood in the shadowy opening.

Fielding swung down from his horse and led it forward. Dunvil did not step out of the doorway. His eyes looked like small beads.

"Mornin'," said Fielding.

"Same to you."

"Heard you were here."

Dunvil scratched his beard but said nothing.

Fielding spoke again. "Bad thing that happened."

"They happen too often."

"Lodge was a good friend of mine."

"I know." Dunvil's hand rose as if he was going to lean against the doorjamb, and then it lowered.

Fielding, in no hurry, took a couple of seconds before going on. "Another friend, named Selby, was the one who found him. Said the deputy's been out here."

"Might have been."

"Said the deputy is askin' around whether anyone knows anything or saw anything."

"Might be."

Fielding paused. Dunvil was being more reserved than he expected, and he did not move from the doorframe. Fielding decided to go ahead. "You didn't happen to see anyone out this way on the day of the shooting, did you?"

"I keep to myself."

"Sometimes those are the people who see things."

"Well, I didn't." The beady eyes held steady.

Fielding thought of another approach.

"Have you been in the house?"

"Not my place." The beard made a strange movement as Dunvil wrinkled his nose. Then he went on. "Maybe you think none of it is. But don't get the wrong idea. I'm not trying to take it."

"I wouldn't think you were."

"Call me the guardian of the dispossessed if you want."

The wording gave Fielding pause. "I'm not questioning your motives," he said.

"I didn't think you would, but make no mistake. This is bigger than the case at hand."

Fielding was not sure how to take the last statement, but he thought it was the anarchist's idea of making an example out of an isolated incident. Hoping to bring the conversation into comprehensible terms, he said, "This outfit called the Argyle seems determined to push out the smaller stockmen, and they don't seem to be holding back now."

Dunvil wagged his head. "Let the overlords come. If they get near me, they'll wish they'd thought twice."

Fielding nodded.

"If they have time to think about it," Dunvil added.

Seeing that he had gotten as much knowledge as he was likely to, Fielding said, "Well, I suppose I'll move along."

"I might, too," said Dunvil. "But not quite so soon."

Fielding mounted up and rode away without looking back. For his own interest, he would have liked to see what Dunvil had inside the stable door, but he was pretty sure it had a stock and a barrel, maybe two.

Fielding rode around and came into the Roe yard from his usual direction. A mélange of noises came from the backyard, and a horse was grazing between two piles of salvage in front. Roe himself was leaning with both forearms against the side of his wagon, which was standing empty beyond the front step of the house. With slow movement, the man stood up from his leaning position and faced his visitor.

He was dressed in his usual fashion, with his worn hat, loose clothes, and cloth vest. Two or three days had passed since his last shave, and the knotted kerchief hung limp at his neck. With thumb and forefinger he lifted the stub of a cigarette to his lips.

Fielding dismounted and held the reins.

Roe's eyes wandered over Fielding and the horse as he lowered the cigarette and said, "How'd'ya do?"

"All right, and yourself?"

"A day older than yesterday, and still a dollar short."

"Isn't that it?" said Fielding.

Roe twisted his mouth and did not offer another comment.

Fielding picked up the conversation. "Things go on. I was over and saw Selby earlier. Just talkin' about things in general. I've got another trip to go on in a couple of days, and I thought I'd check with you others before I take off."

Roe rubbed his face and said, "Not much goin' on right now. I think everyone's sittin' tight after what's happened."

"Seems like. You know, when I talked to Selby a couple of days ago, he was all for stickin' together, but now it looks like he's hunkerin' down."

"Suppose so." Roe lifted the cigarette and smoked it down to the last pinch.

"It's all right with me. I just like to know how things stand."

"Hard to know." The old hat lowered as Roe dropped the cigarette butt and stepped on it. He had his tongue between his lips as he looked up.

Fielding felt as if he was still missing a piece. "Has something else happened, or has this thing with Lodge got everyone down?"

Roe moved his mouth and then spoke. "Maybe either or both."

"Something new, then?"

The pale brown eyes held on him for a few seconds. "That kid Mahoney died yesterday. You know he got shot."

"I heard that, but I also heard no one was sayin' how or where."

"All the same, you don't know whether it's goin' to give them reason to do something more."

Fielding saw it all in a moment. Not only did Selby and Roe not want anything to come back on them, but if they sat tight enough, it might come only to the man who was assumed to have fired the shots at Mahoney. Selby and Roe were all for sticking together when they needed Fielding's help, but now when it looked as if he might be marked, he was on his own. Not only was Lodge's prediction true, but so was another comment that Fielding had not forgotten. Susan Buchanan herself had told him in her polite way that it was not worth it to stick up for people who probably wouldn't do the same for him. And that was the way things stood now.

"Maybe they will try something," Fielding

said. "At least I know more than I did before."

"I thought Bill might have told you."

"No, we didn't get around to that."

"Well, I didn't like the little snot myself. The way he started that fight."

"It wasn't the only one. But I guess he's done now."

"A lot of good it did him." Roe twisted his head in an odd kind of exercise, and then with a quickened tone he said, "Oh, here's Bel."

Fielding turned to see Isabel. She was wearing a dark blue dress and dark shoes, and her hair hung loose as it often did. Her eyes sparkled and her clean teeth showed as she spoke.

"Hello, Tom. I thought I heard voices."

"We were just talkin'," said her father.

"Oh, I'm sorry."

"Nothin' to it."

"That's right," said Fielding. "And I think we were just about done, weren't we?"

"I guess," said Roe. He had taken out his pocketknife and opened it, and now he clicked it shut and put it away.

"It's good you came out," said Fielding. "I was getting ready to leave."

"Well, I can walk along with you as far as the road."

"I won't complain." Fielding looked at Roe, who had taken out his tobacco sack and was opening the drawstring. "Thanks for the talk," said Fielding.

"You bet. Be careful, now."

"I will." Fielding turned the horse and fell in beside Isabel.

After they had walked a few yards, she said, "I'm glad you stopped in today."

He made a smile. "I'm sorry if I'm not in a cheery mood."

"I heard some of it. Papa doesn't want to have much to do with anything, does he?"

"He and Bill Selby both. I guess I can't blame them much."

"They seemed to appreciate your help when they needed it."

"I think they did. But other things have happened since then. Richard Lodge, and then this kid Mahoney. You heard about that?"

Isabel nodded, and the shine of the sun moved on her dark hair. Her eyes had a pained expression and then relaxed.

"I can't say I'm very sorry," Fielding went on. "He was the one who pushed Ed Bracken into the gunfight, and I'm pretty sure he got shot when he opened fire on me and killed my horse."

She put her hand on his arm as they

continued walking. "No one can blame you for that."

"No, but they might want to get even. I think that's part of why Selby and your father want to lie low."

"I'm glad you're not like that."

"Thanks. It's just not a pretty spot to be in."

"You're your own man," she said. "You stick up for yourself. Maybe someone else doesn't like it, but it counts a lot with me."

"Thanks for that, too."

They walked to the end of the lane and turned to each other. Fielding cast a glance toward the yard and saw her father gazing in their direction. With his left hand, Fielding took off his hat and held it as a shield as he leaned forward to kiss her.

As they parted he said, "So long for now. I'll be thinking of you."

"Be careful. And I'll be thinking of you, too."

He led the bay out a few steps, checked the rigging, and swung aboard. He turned in the saddle to wave, and he caught her smile.

The glow stayed with him for a while, but the meetings with Roe and Selby came back to remind him of how things stood. He was on his own now. He had no one to blame.

It was of his own making, and he had to face what would come. This whole feud had moved from push and shove to bullets and blood, and it wasn't likely to go away by itself.

CHAPTER TWELVE

The broad, bladelike part of the needle glinted in the morning sunlight as Fielding pushed the instrument through the canvas. Then he reached around, grasped the tip, and pulled the needle the rest of the way until the thread was tight. He looped the thread over the seam and poked the needle in place again. Tucking his elbow against his side, he moved his right hand so that the eye end of the needle rested in one of the steel pits in the button-like thimble, which was set in a leather strap that ran across his palm. He made sure the needle was straight, then pushed with the heel of his hand until the shiny tip broke through again.

When Isabel had first given him the needle, he thought it might be large and dangerous for his purposes, but now that he was trying it out, he could see it was safer than the smaller one, which sometimes went off course and jabbed him in the finger as he held the fabric.

He worked his way along the seam, repairing the rip in the sheet of canvas. From time to time, the blade of the needle flashed. Fielding imagined a sailmaker, sitting at a workbench in a sunny seaport town, working beneath a blue sky as white sails filled the harbor like so many leaves in an aspen grove. He pictured a bearded sailmaker in a knit cap, with barrels of flour and molasses stacked on the wharves in the background, as in a painting. On the ships in the harbor, sailors pulled on ropes, tied knots. Cowboys of the seas, he had heard them called, weathered men who sang songs as they spliced heavy ropes.

Fielding did not know any seafaring songs except "Little Mohea" and "The Keyhole in the Door," but he knew that many of the songs sung by cowpunchers were based on older versions that came across the ocean. Right now, a fragment of a rangeland song ran through his mind as he worked the stitch.

"At the first break of morning
I'll rise with the day
And gather my horses,
The dun and the gray."

He did not remember where he had heard the song, or if he had heard it all the way through, but this much stayed with him.

After he had finished his mending job and put the needle back in his hatband, he folded the canvas and took it to the gear tent. As he bent over the stack of folded manties, he heard the sound of horse hooves on hard dirt. Drawing his pistol, he went to the tent flap and looked out.

A gray-bearded man, older than Roe or Selby and heavier than either of them, was poking along on a sorrel that Fielding recognized as one from the livery stable in town. He holstered his gun and stepped out into the open.

"Good morning," he said. "Come on in."

The older man rode a little farther, stopped the horse, and with some effort pushed up and over and then lowered himself to the ground. "Top of the mornin' to you," he said.

"Anything I can help you with?" Fielding asked.

"They told me in town you might need a hand."

Fielding noted the man's sagging build and stained suspenders. "I might. How are you around horses?"

The man's left eye squinted at the outer

corner, and muscles on his cheekbone twitched. "Been around 'em all my life."

"Well, that's good. If someone sent you here, then you know what kind of work I do. I'm about to take a load of supplies up into the mountains for a line camp. You know these outfits run cattle up there on summer range."

"Oh, I know all about that. Good for the cattle. They get more shade, more water, better grass. Not so many bugs. Oh, yeah, I've been around."

"What kind of work have you been doin'?"

The man spit to the side. "Plowin' firebreaks for the railroad."

"Is that all done with?"

"No, but if I'm goin' to walk from here to Montana, back n' forth a quarter of a mile at a time, I'd rather do it without a mule fartin' in my face."

"Well, horses aren't much different. You might not have to walk so much on this job, but there's a lot more to it than sittin' in the saddle."

"Oh, you tell me. I was puttin' in fourteen hours a day in the saddle before you were born. Worked hard all my life. I've graded miles of road all by myself, built bridges since I was fifteen."

"I don't doubt it," said Fielding. "What's

your name, by the way?"

"Nate. Last name of Freyer. Nate's good enough."

"Fryer, huh? Last time I had one named Baker."

"Two cooks. Ha-ha!" The man opened his mouth and showed a row of yellow teeth.

"Well, Nate, I'll tell you what. I could use the help, and the company as well. But once we get out there, you pretty much have to stick with it. I expect to be gone for eight to ten days."

"Ah, hell, that don't faze me none. When we was cuttin' logs, we'd be out for a hundred, hundred and twenty days."

"That's fine. What say we give it a try right away, see if things'll work out?"

"Sure."

"How about if you take that brown horse out of the corral and tie him up? You can brush him down, and I'll give you the saddle and blankets. Once you saddle him and get the bridle on, you can take a couple of turns on him."

Nate's left eye twitched, and his right eye opened wide. "He's not a bronc, is he?"

"Oh, no. This is the one I start my wranglers out on."

As Fielding stood by and watched, the older man went to work. He seemed plenty familiar with the routine, and he talked a streak as he went through the tasks. The railroads were going to be the death of the free country, he said. They seemed like a blessing, made it possible to ship cattle to Omaha. But they cut up the country, and they brought out people who could never make it when things were tough. Brought out doors and windows and ice and pianos, so that men who didn't want to work could sing in whorehouses. Brought out machinery to harvest grain, crush rocks. Mill your own lumber to build more towns. And the engines, they scared everything they didn't kill on the tracks. No tellin' how many times horses had spooked, then cut themselves on barbwire and bled to death. "That's another thing they bring, barbwire."

"They sure do," said Fielding.

"That's why I wanta go to the far-look country."

"There's no rails where we'll be goin', that's for sure."

"That's the kind of country I like. You either pack it in, or it don't git there."

"Uh-huh. Can you get three fingers in?"

"You bet." Nate put three fingers between the cinch and the horse's body.

"Here's the bridle, then."

The horse would not open its mouth for

270

the bit, so Fielding put on the bridle. He worked the bit into the mouth and drew the headstall over and behind the ears. After straightening the bridle, he handed the reins to the older man and said, "Let's lead him out a ways, to be clear of everything, and check the cinch again."

Nate led the horse into the broad sunlight and stopped. He seemed to be stalling, as he pulled and picked at the cinches, shook the saddle horn, turned the stirrup this way and that, and led the horse forward a couple more paces. He draped the reins with quite a bit of slack and then had to try a couple of times to get his foot in the stirrup. With a whoosh of breath he grabbed the saddle front and back and began to pull himself up. When he had his weight over the saddle, he moved his right hand from the cantle to the horn, and with continued labor he swung his leg over and settled onto the saddle.

Before he could catch the right stirrup, the brown horse started bucking. It pushed higher with the front quarters than the rear, and it did not seem as if it was trying to throw the rider as much as it was just being uncooperative.

Nate pulled the slack in his reins and hollered, "Whoa! Whoa!"

The horse continued raising its front feet, and Nate pulled back on the reins, so that the horse began to stumble backward as it rose in front. Just before it fell onto its left hip, the older man jumped free and staggered back. Fielding caught him. The reins had pulled out of Nate's hand, so the brown horse fought its way back onto its feet. Fielding moved fast, jumped in front of it, and was able to grab the reins.

"Son of a bitch," said the older man. "Does he do that every time?"

"Not that I've seen. And that's the one the wrangler usually rides."

The eye twitched. "Well, I don't know how much I want to ride him."

"I don't know. We could put you on another one. But like I said, it's a long ways out there and back."

The man raised his chin and looked over the length of the brown horse, then turned to glance at the livery stable horse. "I'm not married to any of this," he said.

"It's not the best work for everyone," Fielding offered.

"I don't think it is for me." Nate pulled up the waist of his trousers. "How often do you go through help?"

"Not countin' you, I had three others since I started this season in May."

"Well, good luck with number four when you find him."

"Thanks. It probably won't be on this trip. I'm supposed to pull out tomorrow."

As Nate and the livery horse rode away out of sight, Fielding pursed his lips. He was no worse off than he had been an hour earlier. He was still on his own.

Fielding rested the horses on a level spot halfway up the switchbacks. The first part of this trip was the hardest, but none of it was easy. The trail ahead, as he remembered it, ran through the bottom of one rock-wall canyon and along the side of another canyon where there was no passage for horses or men in the bottom. On some of the high stretches, there wasn't room to turn around a horse, and the mountainside fell away into dizzying space.

He counted his horses again, out of habit. Seven was as many as he cared to handle by himself, especially in rough country. As for count, it was just as well he didn't have another rider. He needed all seven of these to carry the salt and the camp provisions for the Half Moon as well his own camp and supplies. It took the equivalent of one and a half horses just to carry the grain for a trip like this.

On up the switchback, he came out onto a stretch of trail that ran along the top of a ridge. Here he let three of the horses go on their own. The land broadened out on each side, with timber and deadfall on the right and boulders and grass on the left. Interspersed among the gray rock formations were live trees, mostly pine, with plenty of dead snags and fallen, twisted trunks. The air was fresh here, and he expected it to get chilly at night, so he was glad to see the firewood.

That evening he let the horses graze until nightfall and then tied them up for the night. The wind in the pines sounded like rushing water, and the creaking of trees blended with the shuffle of horse hooves as he rolled out his bed. The night was dark, and the rest of the world seemed far away. At times like this he felt at home in the spareness of what they called the high lonesome.

With daylight he was back to work and business. He knew the way ahead was going to get narrow as it went down and through a canyon with close walls. He tied all seven horses in a line and hit the trail.

The sun was straight overhead when he hit the bottom of the canyon. The trail ran alongside a clear creek, so he took the time to untie the horses and let them drink. Their hooves clattered on the smooth rocks, and the packs rubbed as the horses pushed their way to the water. A light, sucking sound came from the horses drinking. Tails swished. A faint hum of gnats carried on the air when motion ceased. Fielding ate a cold biscuit and a handful of raisins, then drank from his canteen and went upstream to fill it. He splashed water on his face. A few minutes later, he got the horses in line again and led them out.

The path ran level for half a mile and then began to climb. For a while, the trail had crossed and re-crossed the creek a few times, but now the creek stayed on the left. Large boulders rose on the right wherever the canyon wall sat back. The sky above was a swath of blue where hawks and eagles floated in and out of view. The afternoon was warm, and Fielding began to drowse.

He came alert when the horse stopped beneath him. A large man on a tall horse blocked the way in front. The rider and horse seemed taller than they were because of the rise in the trail, but Fielding had them both placed. The man wore a gray hat and black vest, and the sorrel wore a brand of interlocking diamonds. The sight of them gave rise to a feeling of dislike.

"You get around a lot for a sack jig, don't you?" said Fielding.

The sorrel shifted position, and Foote's sidearm came into view. "Who's to say?" asked the man.

"Don't push yourself too far," answered Fielding. "I've got work to do, and you're blocking my way."

"Do you own it?"

"I think we went through this before, but I don't expect you to understand things very fast."

"If you're so smart, why don't you try to make me move?"

"Because you might make a bad choice and hurt yourself with that hog leg."

"If you think I don't —"

"And besides," Fielding cut in, "I want to give you a chance to make good on your threat of the other day."

Foote's eyes opened. "What was that?"

"You said anytime, you and me. I believe you said, 'Fists is my favorite way.' How about it?"

"Here?" Foote's eyes darted to both sides of the trail.

"Not here. There's no room. Turn around, and we'll go up to a wide spot."

"And let you shoot me in the back?"

"Don't be a fool. Why would I want to do that, when I can punch you in the face?" Fielding did not add that he assumed Pence was somewhere not far away, and a gunshot would bring him on the double.

"By God, I'm gonna love rubbin' your face in the dirt."

"Let's see if you can do it."

Foote took the bait and turned his horse around. He set out on a lope. Fielding didn't blame the man for not wanting to leave his back exposed for any longer than he had to, and he might also be following the old rule of being the first to get to the place where they were going to fight.

Fielding rode on, his nervousness building, until he came to a spot on the right side of the trail where Foote had dismounted. The big man had his horse tied to a three-inch pine trunk and had hung his hat, vest, and gun belt on the saddle horn. Fielding came down off his horse and tied it to a tree, then tied the pack string to another. As he hung his hat and his gun belt on his saddle horn, he thought he might have one advantage. He knew he had to come out of this fight intact, and he was going to put everything he had into it. In contrast, he thought Foote was looking for an opportunity to beat up or even cripple his rival, but Fielding did not think the man was committed to the whole Argyle plan, if he even knew of it.

The galoot, as Adler called him, came forward with his fists up. He had his head lifted, and his front teeth showed in the sneering smile he wore. Fielding raised his own fists and came within five feet of his opponent. Each man began to circle to the left. Fielding had the impression that Foote was not as nimble in heeled riding boots as he would like, and he stumbled on a raised root from a pine tree.

Fielding leaned forward and put some spring in his step. He danced in, threw a jab that didn't land, and bounced out. He tried the move a second time, caught the man flat-footed, and came right back in with a punch that landed. Foote came around and squared off, then lunged forward with a left that grazed Fielding's cheekbone. Fielding skipped out of range, bounced to his right, came back to his left, sprang in with a jab, and stepped back out. Foote was taking slow, heavy steps as he followed.

Fielding continued to move back and forth, widening the arc. When he caught the man with one foot almost square in front of the other, he moved straight in and landed three fast punches in a row. As he backed out, Foote rushed him in a charge of fury. Fielding ducked and caught a glancing blow on the right side of the head, then came up and around and hooked a left into Foote's jaw. The big man stumbled, as he had been moving forward and the punch knocked him off course. He came up and around, his weight back on his heels. Fielding rushed him, getting clobbered on the ear as he did, but he succeeded in knocking the man off balance as he stepped backward. Fielding hit him square in the mouth, and the man fell to the ground.

Foote came up to his hands and knees, as if he was trying to think of what to do next, and Fielding took advantage of the moment.

"You can get up if you want," he said, "but you're not going to beat me. The best you'll do is land a few more good ones, but you'll get at least that much back. I don't think you've got it in you to settle it with a gun, but I'm takin' this, just in case." He moved to the man's horse and pulled the .45 Colt from the holster. Then he spoke again. "You might think you could, and you might be able to squeeze off a shot before the whole thing came to you, but let me tell you something. This isn't your game. They took you on, but what they want is another Mahoney. Here's what he did. He picked a fight with my wrangler, Ed Bracken, and shot him down. Then he took some potshots at me, and he got some lead in return. He died of it — infection, blood poisoning, you tell me. But he died miserable and stupid because he wanted to be a hard man. If you want to do that, get yourself another gun and stay on with this outfit. See how far it gets you. But I don't think you want to kill anyone, much less get killed yourself. The best thing you can do is go back where you came from. There's nothin' wrong with it."

Foote stood up. "I hate you. I want to pound you into the dirt."

"That's all right, too. But you don't want to kill me. These others folks would like you to, so you can be their dummy." Fielding went to the buckskin and put the extra six-gun in his saddlebag. As he untied the horse, he said, "Don't follow me. Go back home. As for this, you didn't lose a fight today. You just didn't win."

Foote had a glare in his eyes, but Fielding did not think the man would follow. What made him vain would also help him see that it wasn't worth it.

Fielding sat up late that night, wrapped in his blankets and holding his pistol in his lap. He did not have a fire. Sooner or later,

Pence would come to harass him, he was sure of that. He doubted that Pence would take the chance of getting shot in the night, but he wasn't going to leave the door wide-open. Again he had tied all the horses after letting them graze for a while. He had not set up his sleeping tent because he did not want to shut out any sounds and he did not want to provide a white target. So he sat against a pine tree with his horses around him like a sentry line.

He dozed off and on, fell into longer stretches of sleep. He heard the horses move and snuffle, and the stamp of a hoof would bring him awake. Then he would drift again.

The chattering of a squirrel woke him to the gray sky of morning. He counted the dark shapes of horses. All there. He held still and listened. Then the sound came, the tramp of a deer. Three steps and a pause, four more steps. After another pause, the deer came into the clearing where the horses had grazed the night before. It was a good-sized blacktail with antlers in velvet, one side larger than the other. The buck poked his head forward with each step as he crossed the clearing.

Fielding sat a few minutes more, then tossed the blankets aside and got started on the day. He watered the horses two at a time at the creek bed, where he saw the tracks of the deer pressed into the mud and light gravel. He grained the horses in their feed bags, and as daylight came to the canyon he put on the packsaddles and tied on the loads.

He was used to losing an hour when he had to pack up camp and get all the horses ready by himself, but on this day he wished he had gotten an earlier start. Today's stretch was going to take him up the side of the mountain, and it was going to be a long, hot haul.

Fielding knew where the narrow climb began. He rested the horses, checked all the packs and lashes, and started again. Before long they were going up the worn path of powdery dust and chipped rocks.

The buckskin was surefooted, and he watched the trail. The drop-off to the left did not seem to bother him, and he moved along at a steady pace. Fielding held the lead rope in his left hand and the reins in his right, a little awkward but a good precaution. He hoped he did not have to get down from the horse at any point, such as to roll a rock out of the way, and he hoped most of all not to come upon a snake or a washout.

In many places there was not room to step down and go around a horse. If the buckskin saw a snake and did not spook, Fielding would have to dismount, go as light-footed as possible, and try to get the snake with the shovel. Shooting was out of the question. Unless he had a big rock and a sure target, it was not a good idea to try that method, either. All he would have would be a mad rattler on the side of the trail. If the buckskin saw a snake first and did spook — Fielding did not like to think of that.

In the case of a washout, where the trail ended with a gap too broad to cross, he would have a long ordeal in trying to back eight horses down a narrow trail. There were two ways out of this canyon — the way he had come, and the way he was going. In some places a man might climb up on the right, but Fielding could not see how far. He did know that when he climbed a steep mountain on foot, he could never see very far ahead, and when he thought he was nearing the top, he often learned he still had a long ways to go.

Fielding had plenty to think about, then, as he led the pack string up the side of the mountain. When he had a moment clear, he would turn in the saddle and count the seven shifting packs as the horses labored up the trail.

He thought he was nearing the top, because the ground sloped up and away on his right, and the gap in front was clear sky. If it was the top, he could pull the animals off the trail and let them rest.

The idea vanished when the buckskin jumped and took off in a scramble. The lead rope pulled from Fielding's hand, and he leaned forward to get his balance. He took hold of the reins with his left hand and got the horse stopped. The trail was wide enough, so he jumped down and looked back at this string. The horses were pushing and grunting, jostling the packs on the uphill side of the trail. Fielding heard something like a crashing sound from the canyon below. He thought an elk might have crossed the trail in back of the horses, but then he counted his animals through the thin cloud of dust. A jolt came to the pit of his stomach when he saw that he had only five. The dark horse had gone over and taken the brown with it.

He could see the empty space at the end of the line where the horses should be. This was worse than a hell of a fix. He needed to get these other horses out of the way so he could go back and check on the two that were gone. The thought of edging past five restless animals on a ledge made him uneasy. Dropping the reins of the buckskin, he walked back to the first packhorse, the gray, and pulled the lead rope from where it lay dragging between the horse's feet.

Holding the rope at its knotted end, he led the string of five horses up the trail. He took the reins of the saddle horse in his right hand and kept walking. A quarter of a mile farther, he came out to an open area of rocks and low bushes with timber farther back. He ground-hitched the buckskin and tied the lead rope to a dead log. Then he went back to check on the other two.

The day was warm and still, about straight-up noon. It could take him hours to straighten up this mess, unless the worst had happened and the two horses were a total loss. He walked along the trail, passing the spot where he had gotten off his horse. The ground was plenty marked up from the spooked and crowded horses. Then he found the place where scuff marks went over the edge.

It was a steep drop-off here, and he knelt to look over. He found the packs first, white spots against jagged gray boulders, a good two hundred feet below. The dark horse lay belly-up, and the brown horse was on its right side with its head downhill out of view. Both horses were motionless, and Fielding was trying to calculate whether it was worth the time and effort of going down the cliff to salvage the panniers and what was left of the Half Moon's camp grub.

He heard the crunch of footsteps and the jingle of spurs.

Pushing back from the verge, he stood up and turned to see the blocky form and tall hat of George Pence.

"What's got you stuck, packer?" Pence kept walking forward.

"What's it look like?"

Pence did not stop, but he slowed down. "Looks to me like you lost somethin'."

"Not without help."

"Maybe you'd like some help gettin' down there with 'em — Nah, nah. Don't touch that gun, or I'll have to go for mine. Make a lot of noise, put a hole through you."

That was the plan, Fielding thought. To throw him over without putting a hole in him would make it look like an accident. It might look suspicious, but it wouldn't call for an investigation. Fielding moved from the middle of the trail toward the bank on the uphill side.

Pence came forward, his hand hovering over the butt of his gun.

Fielding held his right hand up and out, his left up and closer to his hat. He could see Pence's side whiskers in the shade of the hat brim, and he could see the dull eyes keeping track of the raised right hand as he closed in.

Fielding's left thumb and first two fingers found the head of the needle in his hatband. His right hand stayed free as a decoy. As Pence raised his arms and moved in for the bear hug, Fielding pulled out the four-inch needle and plunged the blade into the center of Pence's abdomen, right below the spot where the ribs met. After a second, he pulled the needle back.

The eyes widened in the beefy face as Pence straightened up and drew back, his arms widening and falling away. Fielding hit him with everything he could put into a right punch. Dropping the needle, he followed with a left. Pence seemed to be dazed but stayed on his feet, moving back a few inches with each heel. Then he gasped a breath and lunged forward, mauling with his big fists until he caught Fielding on the left side of the head and knocked his hat off.

Fielding pulled back to avoid another punch. He ducked, moved, and came up. Pence seemed to be fighting on instinct, coming after his opponent with sheer power. Fielding went low, came in under the taller man's grasp, and drove his shoulder into

Pence's midsection. The man let out a groan of pain and slammed a fist into Fielding's kidney area. Fielding lifted with his shoulder, pushed back, and sent the big man sprawling on the ground. The tall hat rolled aside, and Pence struggled onto his left elbow.

Fielding saw a small dark spot forming on the man's shirt, but he knew he couldn't wait and see whether Pence was bleeding inside. He piled on as the man's right hand moved toward his pistol butt.

Pence reached up and grabbed Fielding's chin between his thumb and fingers. With his left hand he reached for Fielding's hair and closed his fingers.

Fielding smashed at the heavy face and pulled back, getting his head free. Then he pushed up and away, ready for Pence to rise.

He did not think Pence knew how close he was to the edge, for the man got his legs under him and took half a step back as he came up. He had nothing but a backdrop of empty air as Fielding planted a foot and feinted.

Pence raised his fists and stepped back, then clawed the air as he fell out of view.

Fielding stood away from the edge, pulling in deep breaths and trying to steady his hands by leaning over and placing them on his knees. In a couple of minutes he felt calmed down enough to look over.

Pence lay a ways uphill from the rest of the wreck. He was sprawled out facedown with his head turned to the side.

Fielding stepped back again, found Pence's high-crowned hat, and sailed it over the edge. After picking up his own hat, he looked for the needle until he found the shiny blade in the dirt. As he poked the instrument back into his hatband, he thought, it was just a little hole, and it didn't go all the way through.

CHAPTER THIRTEEN

Up on top again with his remaining horses, Fielding sat on a log to collect himself. He drank from his canteen and wished he could find a place to wash up. The horses nearest to him, the buckskin and the gray, showed no curiosity, but he knew he was dirty, bruised, scraped, and disheveled. When he had rested awhile, he stood up and brushed himself off with the flat of his hand. He tucked in his shirt and straightened his trouser legs, then rubbed his face downward with his hands. He had to get going again.

Of the many thoughts that crossed his mind as he rode along, one was that Pence had picked a good place for his sabotage. The drop-off was as steep as anywhere along the trail, and the rocks at the bottom would do what the initial fall didn't. If Fielding had wanted to go down in there, he would have had to descend from farther up or down the trail and then pick his way through a boulder field. From there he would have had to carry anything he wanted to salvage. He supposed at least one of the two crossbuck packsaddles had been smashed, and even if he were able to haul out some of his gear, he would have to leave it somewhere near the trail until he came back this way. As for the cow camp supplies, he was sorry for that loss, and he did not know how much of it he could recover or would be willing to carry up out of the canyon.

He could think about the practical considerations because he had to, because he was in business and had obligations. But as soon as he let in the additional circumstance of Pence's body being down there, the whole prospect became even less feasible. He did not want to be picking through dead horses, mangled gear, and ruptured flour sacks with a dead man nearby drawing flies. Furthermore, he would make a good target down there, while his saddle horse and pack animals were up here. Putting all these things together, he decided to call it a complete loss and leave things as they were, for someone else to figure out. Meanwhile, he still had goods to deliver.

The men at the Half Moon cow camp did

not ask questions, and Fielding did not elaborate. He said he lost two horses with full loads in a canyon the day before, and they said they could get by for a while on what he had come through with. He ate dinner of fried venison with them as his horses rested, and in the early afternoon he started back. That night he camped in the same place as the night before, in a stand of timber about a mile off the trail. He was getting used to not having a fire, and he didn't need to camp near water if he was going to keep the horses tied up all night.

In the morning he got a good start on the day, as he was traveling light and had fewer horses than he did a couple of days earlier. He watered the stock when he came to a stream, and then he moved on.

At midmorning he came to the spot where he had rested with the horses after the fight with Pence. He stopped this time as well, letting the animals take a breather before he took them on the narrow trail down the mountainside. After a short while, he got them moving again.

His practical tendencies had not let go. For the last two days he had been nagged by a sense that he should try to go down and recover some of his equipment after all. But when he came around a bend in the trail and saw buzzards floating above the chasm, not much more than a stone's throw straight out from the ledge, he chose to ride past without even looking over.

Going down a grade such as this one was slow and tiring, even with light packs. Fielding came out at the bottom in early afternoon, and half a mile farther he found a place where he could take the horses to the creek. The water was backed up with a pool here, as a result of debris from the gorge piling up against the rocks and a fallen log. Waterside bushes grew up out of the damp sand, and green scum lay along the edge of the water. Insects skimmed across the surface, and greenish yellow bee flies buzzed a foot above the slime. The horses drank. Fielding listened for noises out of place but heard none, only the flow of water and the shifting of horses.

He envied the animals for their ability to ignore everything but the moment. He could remember a time, not so long ago, when he, too, could take things a step at a time and not be burdened with thoughts of what he had come through and what lay ahead. Maybe he could do that again. He did not know. At present he had all too clear a sense that two horses and a man lay bloating in a sunbaked canyon upstream from here, and a boss down in the valley would want to know how things had gone.

Fielding listened again. It was quiet here, sometimes too quiet. He recalled stories of men who stayed too long in the mountains and heard trains. It was something to laugh at in this far country of mules, horses, and shank's ponies. Fielding had been content to haul merchandise he could lift onto a horse's back, and he had been happy to leave the railroad far behind. Trains, as he had heard a few days earlier, brought machinery and pianos so that men could crush rocks and sing in whorehouses. Now here he was in the mountains, where he was supposed to be able to get away from the weight of civilization, and it seemed as if he was packing it right along with him.

Most of the horses had their muzzles up, so he lined them out and got them going again. The travel was easier now, still downhill but not steep. If he made good time, he would have to spend only one night more in the mountains. After that, he would decide what to do with himself and his work.

He pushed on through the afternoon and early evening. Shadows were deepening as he came out of the rock-wall canyon. When the country opened up again, he watered the horses and took them off the trail as before. One more dry camp without fire, one more night sitting up and catching sleep as it came, did not figure as a great hardship. As a way of life, though, it did not promise much.

The sunlight warmed his face as he started the climb the next morning. The trail was wider here, with timber, rocks, and grass on either side. He knew he would be traveling up and along the ridge of a line of mountains, with plenty of dips and rises. When he came to the last promontory looking out over the plains, he would still have the switchbacks to go down.

The horses moved at a fast walk, and each time he looked back, he saw the dust rising from their passage and floating in their wake. Looking forward, he recognized some places and not others. The trail always looked different going one way than it did on the return, even though he had the habit of looking back at the country as he traveled.

The farther he went along the ridge, the less hospitable the north side of the trail became, as it fell away in rock slides and steep timbered slopes. Water was harder to find up here, as it did not often cross the trail in the form of a stream, but there were places on the mountainsides where water collected in tarns and ponds. He kept an eye out for such watering places, riding from time to time to the edge of the wide back of the mountain and looking down the slope to the south. At midday he found a pool and took the horses there to drink.

Most of the horses had finished drinking, and the sorrel was sloshing water backward with its chin, when Fielding heard a voice in back of him. He turned to see a dark-haired rider who was not wearing a hat. As the person waved, Fielding realized it was Isabel. He waved for her to come down the hill.

"What a surprise," he called out as she came near.

"Lucky that I found you." Her teeth showed as she smiled. "I just happened to look down this way, and I thought it was you with all these packhorses."

He saw that she was wearing a work shirt and a pair of trousers, and she had a small bag tied onto the back of her saddle. "This is a long ways from home for you," he said. "More than a day's ride."

As she climbed down from her horse, she said, "I stayed overnight in Wheatland."

He gave her a closer look. "What does your father think of that?"

"I don't know. I left him a letter saying I had to get a message to you."

"Really? What is it?"

The smile faded from her face. "Tom, Leonora told me that she heard Cronin's men were going out to look for you."

"Well, they found me. At least, two of them did. One of them ought to have made it back by now. Even if he wanted to keep on riding, he would have to turn in his horse."

She frowned. "Who was that?"

"The sometimes cowpuncher Ray Foote."

An expression of distaste came over her face. "I heard he went to work for them. What was he doing out here?"

"I think he had an idea of thrashing me."

"Did he get very far?"

"Not very. After a scuffle, I told him he was in the wrong game. I took his gun from him, to keep us both safe."

"That's good. And you think he went home?"

"I hope so. He'll do better in his own element. Big man among the punkin rollers. These others play a hard game."

Her eyebrows tightened. "You said two men came out. Was the other one with him?"

"No, he showed up the next day. He spooked two of my horses over the side of a cliff, I think by throwin' rocks. I lost both of them. Then I believe he wanted to send me over the same way."

"But he didn't."

"It was either him or me." Fielding looked to either side. "I'd think they would have sent someone to look for him by now. That's why I'd like to get out of these mountains today if I can."

"I haven't seen anyone."

"Neither have I, until you came along, but it's easy enough for someone to hide out in the timber." He looked at her horse, which he recognized as one of her father's, and then brought his eyes to meet hers. "How about you? Are you tired, or are you ready to turn around and go right back?"

"It's all right with me," she said.

"Good. I'll get these fellows lined up. But first, let me give you this extra gun. Don't pull it out unless you're sure you can use it. Do you know how to shoot one?"

She nodded, then watched him as he took the .45 from his saddlebag and put it in hers.

"You can hold this lead rope if you'd like," he said. He smiled and added, "First step to makin' you a wrangler."

Her eyes sparkled as she smiled and took the rope.

He brought the dun horse around and began tying it to the back of the gray horse's packsaddle. "I don't know what to expect," he said. "Maybe nothing will happen. If something does, you get out of here as fast as you can. One shot, and you light out on a run."

"Even if you're hurt?"

"Don't stick around and gawk. If someone shoots at me, whether he hits me or not, he's not going to want witnesses."

"How about your horses?"

He brought the white horse into line and tied it. "I'll worry about them. I've got fewer than I started with anyway."

"You lost one earlier as well, didn't you?"

"That's right. I'm not doin' well in profit and loss this year, but that doesn't mean as much at the present as getting you and me out of these mountains." He led the bay horse around.

She winced as she said, "Then I'm just in the way."

"That's all right. You did what you thought you should. The main thing is, look out for yourself if anything happens." He turned to fetch the sorrel, but her voice stopped him.

"Tom, I came here because I love you."

He went to her, took her in his arms, and kissed her. "I love you, too, darling. We just need to get out of here all right." He kissed her again, then released her and went for the sorrel, which was near at hand. "I'm going to lead all five of these," he said as he tied the last horse into place. "If you don't mind, you can ride in back. If the dust gets too thick, you can either sag back or come around up front, but I think the safest place is where you don't have anything behind you."

"Tom."

"Yes?"

"When you said it was either him or you —"

He moved his head side to side. "It was their bully, George Pence. He died when he hit the bottom."

She let out a sigh of relief. "That's good to know. I just wanted to make sure I understood."

Back on the trail, Fielding moved the string along at a good pace. By now he was used to counting only five horses when he turned in the saddle, but he still saw the empty spaces at the end where the other two horses should be. Isabel rode a ways back, reining her horse from time to time to avoid the thickest dust.

The trail continued going up and down

and curving around, according to the lay of the land here on top. Fielding was thinking ahead about the switchbacks, when the trail went around a rock formation on the right and a man stepped forward with a rifle.

At first glance, Fielding thought the man might be a road agent from his method of presenting himself and keeping his face in shadow, but after a couple of seconds Fielding realized that the man was Al Adler, wearing a dark gray shirt instead of his customary white. The brown gloves looked like part of his body, and the man's whole bearing was sinister.

In the time that it took Fielding to make the recognition, he had stopped his horse and the pack string. He raised his right hand, hoping that Isabel would heed it and not ride around to catch up with him. From the instant he had seen the rifle, he knew there was no good prospect in making a run for it, and now he hoped Isabel would stay out of sight.

Still in the first few seconds, he took in the immediate scene. Adler had stepped out of an enclosure of gray rocks that rose from the trailside and sloped up to a height of about eight feet, leveled off, and rose again to a dome of fifteen to twenty feet. From there it sloped gradually to the ground on the left. The twisted remains of a tree long ago uprooted lay in the foreground, also on Fielding's left, while a ways past it, standing by itself, a dead snag rose about ten feet in the air with one dead branch sticking out like a withered claw. Coming back to Adler, he saw the tops of dark green cedar trees between the first layer of rocks and the dome, which led him to believe there might be a passageway where Adler had been peeping out on the other side.

The packhorses were snuffling and exhaling, and dust was still drifting, when Adler spoke.

"Good afternoon, Fielding."

"The same to you." Fielding went to lower his hand.

"Keep your arm up there for a minute."

"What's the trouble?"

"You are, as if you didn't know."

"Did your man Foote make it back all right?"

"Don't worry about him."

"If you're lookin' for Pence, he's farther back in, waitin' for you."

"I know where he is."

Fielding doubted what the man said. He wouldn't have had time to go that far and back unless he had left the ranch shortly after Pence did, in which case he would not have come all the way back here to stage this meeting. "If you go there," said Fielding, "you might want to keep an eye out for his horse. Probably wandering around with a set of broken reins."

"You don't know everything you think you do," said Adler. "But it doesn't matter much."

"You're probably right, on the last point at least. Anything I know, someone else does."

The tip of the rifle came up a couple of inches. "Like what?"

"Like you say, it doesn't matter much."

While he was talking, Fielding was glad not to hear anything from behind the pack string. He hoped Isabel had taken cover.

"Enough of that anyway," said Adler. "Here's what we're going to do. Tuck that lead rope under your leg for a minute, and pull your gun out of the holster. Don't get anywhere near the trigger. Hold it out at arm's length, and drop it on the ground."

With slow, deliberate movents, Fielding did as he was told.

Adler continued with his orders. "Now put both hands on the saddle horn, and come down off that horse. When you get down, come around front. I don't want to have to shoot up everything, but I will if it comes to it."

The lead rope fell to the ground as Fielding rose from the saddle and dismounted. His rifle stock was out of reach on the other side of the horse, and he wished he had left Foote's pistol in his own saddlebag. He thought of trying to turn the buckskin, but he believed Adler's threat that he wouldn't scruple to put a bullet through the horse.

As Fielding came around the front of the buckskin, he held on to the reins. He could see his pistol ten feet away in the dirt, but he knew it would be fatal if he made a dive for it. Furthermore, dirt in the gun might cause it to jam.

Adler motioned with the rifle, and the gloved hands gave an impression of complete control. "Drop the reins and step over here," he said.

In that instant, Fielding saw movement beyond where the man stood with the rifle. Isabel had come through the cleft in the rocks where the dark cedar trees grew.

Fielding did not budge. "I don't understand," he said.

Adler's face tensed as he said, "What part? I said drop the reins, and get over here."

Fielding still did not move. He heard the click of a revolver, then Isabel's voice.

"You'd better drop the rifle, mister."

As Adler turned and took a step back, still keeping an eye on Fielding, Isabel came into view. She was holding the .45 with both hands, and she stepped around so that Fielding was not in her line of fire.

"It's a girl," said Adler, stepping toward her.

"I said drop it." Isabel held the gun pointed at him, but it wavered.

Adler took another step. "I think I know you," he said. Then, with a quick backhand swing of the rifle, he knocked the gun from Isabel's hand.

The .45 roared, and the bullet split the air as it passed a couple of yards to Fielding's left. The buckskin jumped, but Fielding held on to the reins. The packhorses were shoving each other and trying to stampede, and both Isabel and Adler were scrambling for the fallen gun. Isabel got her hand on it, and Adler gave her a shove. The pistol clattered out of reach again. As Adler went after it, Fielding pulled the rifle from the scabbard and let the buckskin go.

"Run!" he hollered, hoping that Isabel would remember that she was to get out of the way if a shot was fired.

But she didn't. She picked up a rock the size of both of her hands, raised it, and heaved it at Adler's head. It glanced off his left shoulder but knocked him off course enough that Isabel made another try for the gun. When she did, Adler grabbed her lower leg and gave it a yank.

As she fell on her side, Adler reached for the .45 and got a grasp on it. With the pistol in his gloved right hand and the rifle in his left, he rose and turned, locating Fielding as he did so. The Colt blasted as a concussion of air walloped the left side of Fielding's head.

He knew he had this one second in time, while Adler was standing in the clear. Fielding had the rifle up, and he lined the sights on the center of the dark gray shirt. Everything came together, and he squeezed the trigger.

The Colt fired into the air as Adler jerked backward. The rifle fell at his side, and the pistol went back with his hand and then fell.

Fielding took slow, cautious steps as he approached the man. A dark circle had appeared on the front of the shirt, and the body made no movement.

Isabel had come to her feet and now stood by his side as she spoke. "Is this one Adler?"

"It sure is. I didn't recognize him at first, because he usually wears a white shirt and a brown vest. But that was just for a second."

"Is he the last one?"

"I don't know."

"What do we do, then?"

Fielding cast another glance at the body. "I think we'll leave him here. They'll come looking for him."

"His horse is tied in back of these rocks," she said.

"Well, we should let it go."

He followed her through the gap in the rock, then around to the back of the dome. When they came to the horse, he recognized it.

"See this?" he said. "A dark horse, with no white markings. Black slicker tied on back. This fellow Adler was fitted out for work." Fielding untied the horse, then knotted the reins and slipped them over the saddle horn. "Whoever comes for Adler will find the horse. I didn't think to look for Pence's until much later."

As Fielding and Isabel walked back to the trail, she asked, "And now?"

He held the rifle at his side as he looked around. "We pick up our things, gather the horses, and get going again." He stopped and let his eyes meet hers. "Isabel, I'm sorry you had to see this."

"Sorry? Tom, he had every intention of killing you."

"Well, he didn't get to. I have you to thank

for that. I'll tell you, I'm not used to having someone stick up for me."

She put her hand around his neck and said, "You do now."

CHAPTER FOURTEEN

The song of the meadowlark made the plains seem like a benevolent place as Fielding led the two horses from water back to camp. Isabel's full, dark hair cascaded around her shoulders where she crouched to roll up the gear tent. She pushed up from the bundle and brushed her hands against each other. Her eyes were shining as she met Fielding, close, and put her hand on his waist.

After the kiss, he said, "If you'd like to hold these horses like a good wrangler, I can start getting them ready."

She gave him a lingering smile as she took the first lead rope. "This is a nice-looking one," she said. "I like the coloring on him."

"It's called a dun. Some of these others have a dark mane and tail, but this one's got these other dark spots as well — shadowing on the neck and shoulder, dark ear tips, shadowy face, and of course this stripe running all along the back. Plus the dark hocks and barring on the knees."

"I like him."

"So do I. He's a good horse, never gives any trouble." He handed her the other lead rope. "Here. I'll get a brush."

As he went to work on the dun, with Isabel standing close by, words came easy. "Like I said yesterday, I've had some setbacks. This is hard business, losing three horses the way I did. Always lookin' over my shoulder. But I got myself into it."

"You haven't had much help."

He shrugged. "Not worth complaining about. I think I just have to accept my losses, go back to the valley, and decide on what to do next." He met her eyes. "I don't know what your father will say."

"I'm old enough to be on my own. He can't take the key and lock me up. And besides, he knows that I know that he wouldn't stick with you but just looked out for himself."

Fielding did not speak for a moment. He didn't mind having that kind of an advantage, but he didn't want to say it out loud. So he said, "I've done what I could. And going back to the other point, I think I've had enough of being in the middle of this whole mess. But I need to see what things look like when we get back."

When they had all the horses fitted out, they set off across the grassland. After coming down the switchbacks late in the afternoon the day before, they had ridden six or seven miles on a gentle downhill slope between two lines of hills. They came to water at dusk. Now in broad daylight, Fielding picked out the landmarks again and set a course across country. He led four horses and let the sorrel travel on its own. Isabel rode next to him.

They traveled southeast, leaving the town of Wheatland well to their left. Their path took them through rolling plains country, treeless except for the watercourses. By early afternoon they came to the hills overlooking the valley, and Fielding began to feel apprehension creeping into him. When they came to Antelope Creek about a mile north of his customary camp site, they stopped to rest in the shade and let the horses water.

Isabel crouched at the water's edge and washed her face with small handfuls of water. When she stood, she still looked fresh in spite of several hours of sun and dust.

She came to stand by him. "You look worried," she said.

"I don't know what to expect."

She smiled. "I'll talk to him first. Don't fret."

"Oh, it's not just that. It's this bigger thing as well. I don't know how much trouble Cronin wants to go to."

"He ought to be running low on thugs, shouldn't he?"

Fielding let out a weary breath. "You'd think so, but there's always more to be had."

"You're not worried about Cedric, are you? I think the worst he would do would be to hit someone with a hairbrush."

Fielding laughed. "That might be. But never rule him out. I wasn't thinking of him, though. Cronin got Adler from somewhere, and there's more like him. That's Cronin's style, keep himself in the clear."

Isabel put her hand around Fielding's neck and kissed him. "I think he's got to be running out of steam."

"We'll just have to see."

As they crested the last hill northwest of the Roe place, a hawk rose from the grass with a snake in its talons. The bird flapped away with the pale underside of the reptile trailing in the air. Isabel and Fielding looked at each other and smiled.

Down the hill and into the yard they rode. Isabel went into the house by herself as she had said she would. A few minutes later, she came out.

"I think you can come back either later today or tomorrow," she said. "He's not in a good mood, but I don't think there's anything to worry about." She smiled at Fielding but did not come close as she took the reins of her horse from him.

"That's all right," he said. "I'll take these horses back to the place where I stay, and then I've got a couple of other things to do."

Fielding set up his camp and put out his horses for a while as he got cleaned up. The afternoon shadows were beginning to stretch out when he gathered the horses. He saddled the bay for himself and led the white horse bareback.

He rode into Selby's place in less than half an hour. A breeze riffled in the young cottonwoods as Selby came out and met him in the yard. After the preliminary greetings, Selby asked how Fielding's trip had gone.

"I had some trouble," Fielding answered.

"With your horses? With the weather?"

"With some of the Argyle men. First it was Foote, and he left. Then it was Pence, and Adler after that. I had it out with both of them."

Selby stared and did not speak. His ruddy

313

face looked as if he had things to say and was holding them in.

Fielding went on. "I've had time to think about it, and I've decided I've had enough of these kinds of problems."

Selby nodded, and his light blue eyes held on Fielding. "I don't blame you. It hasn't been easy on anyone."

A wave of resentment came up, and Fielding stifled it. The less said, the better.

Selby spoke again. "I think everything's going to blow over, though."

"I wouldn't know. If they wanted to get even for Mahoney, they might for these other two as well."

"Oh, I don't think anyone's interested in gettin' even at this point."

"How's that?"

Selby's eyes opened wide. "Oh, I guess you haven't heard yet."

"No, I haven't. I just got back, and you're the first person I've talked to."

"Well, big doin's," Selby began. "This comes by way of Ray Foote."

"I would have thought he went home."

"Well, he was goin' to, but Cronin asked him to go out on one little job before he drew his pay." Selby moistened his lips and continued. "Seems that Cronin had heard about the wild man livin' out on Richard's place, and Cronin didn't like it. He wanted the Magpie for a line camp. So he went out there with Ray and Cedric alongside."

"That must have been a good show of force."

"Not so much. According to Ray, the crazy man came out of the stable, and as soon as he found out who Cronin was, he went into a rant about how Cronin had had a man killed and was trying to steal his place. Cronin said somethin' high-handed, and the crazy man reached inside the door of the stable and came out with a shotgun. He blew Cronin right out of the saddle, and those other two lit out at a dead run."

"Whew!" said Fielding. "Just like that."

"How I heard it. They got up a party to go out there later, and the crazy man was long gone. They brought back the body, of course."

"When did this happen?"

"Yesterday."

"Huh." That would have been about the time Adler made his way into the mountains.

Selby's face brightened. "So like I said, I think things are going to blow over."

Fielding tensed again. "Well, that's fine. But I've still had enough. I'm going to get my things together, and I might not be long for this place."

Selby glanced at the white horse, and with a dubious tone he asked, "Did you come for your tent?"

"Not right now. I've got to pick up a saddle in the livery stable in town, and I can tie the tent onto it when I come back through."

"Oh."

"But I did come for something."

"What's that?"

"Richard's two horses. I think I should leave them where he would want them to go."

Selby's eyes widened. "Where would that be?"

"With Leonora."

On the ride into town, Fielding mulled over the news about Dunvil and Cronin. He found it amusing to imagine Cedric jolting away on a fast horse, but a lesser part of the story was interesting to consider as well. Cedric must feel as if he had been left high and dry. His sponsor was gone, the object of his attentions had been taken away, and the Argyle had taken a big drop in status.

Thinking of Susan Buchanan led Fielding to another speculation. Her father must have known trouble was coming. He must have wanted to keep from being drawn in as well as to remove his daughter from the company of someone in Cronin's camp. The big augers were supposed to stick together, but Joseph Buchanan had looked out for himself. In that respect he was not much different from Henry Steelyard or even Selby and Roe.

When Fielding took the matched sorrels to the house where Leonora stayed, she came outside. Her face was lined and weary, and her brown hair was combed and pinned back. The glow of the setting sun colored her cheeks as she looked at the horses with an uncertain expression.

"I don't know what I could do with them," she said.

"You don't have to decide right away. I can leave them at the livery stable for you. The saddles go with them."

She gave a faint shrug, and her eyes tightened.

Fielding said, "I think Richard would want you to have them."

Tears filled her eyes. "Richard was a good man. Everyone else in this valley was so stuck on his own self-interest that I thought Richard was the last good man on earth." She blinked, and her eyes stayed moist. "Now I can see he wasn't. Thank you, Tom."

He had to clear his throat to speak.

"You're welcome, Leonora. I wish you all the best."

Her lips moved, and then she spoke. "The same to you, Tom."

Fielding turned into the lane at Roe's place at midmorning. He was riding the buckskin and leading the other five. The dun was saddled for riding, and the remaining four carried all his belongings and gear.

Andrew Roe came out from the house and stood in the front yard, rubbing his face and waiting for Fielding to come to a stop. When Fielding swung down from his horse, Roe said, "Looks like you're packed up again. Off on another job?"

"Not today." Fielding looked at the stubbled face, but the pale brown eyes did not hold steady. When they came back, Fielding spoke again. "I think I'm done here. Had enough of all this, and gonna move on."

Roe's eyebrows lifted as he said, "Oh." He glanced down the line. "Bel said you lost a couple of horses."

"I did. Three altogether."

Roe pushed out his lower lip and put his hands in his pockets.

When it seemed as if the man was not going to speak, Fielding asked, "Is she around?

I wouldn't mind talkin' to her."

"Oh, sure." Roe turned and went on his slow way to the house.

Isabel came out a minute later, dressed in a clean white blouse and a pair of dark blue corduroy trousers. She tossed her wavy dark hair, and with a much lighter tone than her father's she said, "Good morning, Tom. I'm glad you came by."

"It's good to see you."

She glanced at the string of horses. "Are you on your way somewhere?"

He had thought through his words several times, but nervousness still got in the way. "I guess so. Well — yes, I am. Like I said to your father and Bill Selby before that, I've had enough. There's only one thing keepin' me here, and that's you. I'm not walkin' away from you. If I need to, I can come back."

Her eyes showed concern, but she did not seem flustered. "Where do you have in mind to go?"

"I'm not sure. Generally, north and west. I know I can find work anywhere I go." As his eyes met hers, he could tell she was not troubled at all. His words came easier. "It seems like I've been on the move so much, and after a while a person thinks he'd like to try stayin' in one place. That's it. I'd like to have a place of my own. It doesn't have to be much."

She had come a step closer. He could tell she had had a bath, as she smelled like dark cedar. Her eyes were shining as she said, "It's what you make of it, what it means to you."

This was his moment. He took a deep breath and went on. "I might never have much to show for myself, but whatever I make, I'll do it without running over the top of someone else, or beating another man out of what he's got. It's one way of being free — that, and not having to make up to the bigwigs. If you think you can live with that, we can try boiling our coffee in the same pot."

She gave him a soft smile. "Did you think I would say no?"

He tipped his head. "Not really. I just didn't know if you wanted me to come back later, after I had a place, or a definite situation, or whatever."

She stepped back and looked over his string of horses again. "This looks good enough to go on," she said.

He couldn't be sure he had heard what he did. It seemed as if all the tension he had ever felt had broken away. "Are you sure?" he asked.

"I was waiting for you to come back."

"Do you mean that — ?"

"If you can wait a few minutes, you'll see for yourself." She gave him a light kiss, then turned and walked to the house.

As he waited for what seemed like more than a few minutes, all of the clutter of Roe's seemed cheery. The falling-in shed, the heaps of barbed wire and posts, the hulks of wagons — all of these things that used to weigh on him now seemed like old friends. If the gray geese had come out, he would have expected them to waddle up to him and wait to be petted.

The scuff of the door sounded, and Isabel came out into the sunlight with a satchel in each hand. Fielding could tell she had been crying, but she had her chin up and was smiling.

"Is everything all right?" he asked.

"Oh, yes. We talked about it last night and again this morning. But still, it took a few minutes."

She handed Fielding her bags, and he put them in the panniers of the bay horse. As he snugged the lash rope, he asked, "Is he going to come out and see you off?"

She shook her head. "He's a little moody right now. Everything will be all right when we come back."

Fielding handed her the reins to the dun and gave her a boost to help her into the saddle. When she nodded ready, he swung onto the buckskin.

They rode straight north out of the yard, across the trail, and onto the grassland. As they climbed a hill, the hoot of a train rose from the valley. They paused and turned the horses to take a last look at the town of Umber, and then they went on their way through the great rangeland, side by side, with the string of four horses behind them.